# Tae's

# Place 2

## S. MILLER

ISBN-13: 978-1086413212

## DEDICATION

This book is dedicated to all of my fellow creatives. Keep creating and inspiring others through your art. Even though everyone won't understand you or your vision, know your worth, and never dim your light.

# AUTHOR'S NOTE

As always, I want to start by thanking God for giving me a story to tell and the ability to tell it. While writing TP2, I felt so much pressure. Most of it was from myself, as I really wanted to wrap up Tae's story in the best way possible. This book will always have a special place in my heart, because it helped me realize how good God is. If people knew what this process was like for the second time around, they would be asking me why I didn't quit. There were so many road blocks that could've prevented me from getting this book out, but God's plan is God's plan.

God always finds a way of placing the right people in your life. With that being said, I want to give a huge thank you to my graphic artist, P. You are so amazing, and I love you for coming out of retirement yet again, to create another beautiful cover. I also want to thank all of my friends, family, and supporters. You all give me so much motivation, and I will forever appreciate it.

# CHAPTER 1

"Trell, if you don't go at least 60 on this highway, I'm gonna put my foot in your ass!" I screamed.

It had been a long pregnancy, and as grateful as I was for a successful pregnancy, this little girl had overstayed her welcome. I was over the back pains, swollen feet, and constant trips to the bathroom. Now, these contractions were tearing me up. They were no joke, and every time I looked at Trell, I wanted to fight him for doing this to me. Then to add insult to injury, he wanted to drive slow on the freeway, as if his child wasn't splitting me in half.

Excruciating pain aside, I was ready to meet my baby girl. I hadn't even seen her yet, and I just knew she was beautiful. I was more than ready to love on her. Not only because she was my daughter, but because of what she meant to me. My little girl was the beginning to me finally having the family I'd always wanted.

My whole life I dreamed of this and the more I thought about my little family, the more I thought about the strained relationship with my mother and uncle. Of course, they were around for my gender reveal and my baby shower, but other than that, we hadn't spoken much. It was mostly general conversation about the pregnancy with my mother, and business with Uncle Leon. He relocated to Charlotte permanently because he felt like I needed his protection. It's funny that he felt I need some protection from some unknown assailant, but let me grow up with knowing that I desperately wanted to meet my siblings. I'd tried so hard to get over it, but there was so much that I didn't understand. At this point, I didn't even want to hear any more excuses from them, I just wanted to be back on good terms. I knew my mother was on her way down here to see the baby, and was definitely going to clear the air before she left. I hated not speaking to her, and this had gone on for long enough. In the meantime, I needed to focus on the child that was tearing my up from the inside out. I wished someone had told me it would be this painful.

By the time Trell got me to the hospital, I felt like my entire uterus was being ripped out of my body. He pulled up outside of the maternity ward entrance, and ran around to get me out of the car.

"We're here, babe." He said, "Grab on to me so I can help you walk in."

"Walk!" I screamed, "My ass isn't walking anywhere."

"I'll carry you then." He replied, trying to pick me up.

"Don't touch me!" I yelled, while swatting at him. "The reason we're here now is because you can't keep your damn hands to yourself"

"Tae, how am I supposed to get you in there?"

I screamed, "Go inside and get a damn wheel chair!"

Trell ran inside to do as he was told. I hated to yell at him like that, but I'd have to apologize later. I had a tiny human coming out of me any second now and he was trying to get me to walk in the hospital. It was the middle of august and it was too hot for this shit. He had me all the way fucked up if he thought I was walking anywhere. Seconds later, he came out of the hospital with a wheelchair and a nurse in tow. They got me out of the car, and wheeled me back to one of the triage rooms.

"I need drugs now!" I yelled at the nurse.

"We're going to check you in, and get you back to a labor room. You can get an epidural there."

I tried not to think about the pain I was experiencing, but I felt like I was about to split in half. They were moving a little too slow if you asked me, but the nurses kept telling me that I would be fine. Once they got me in the room, a nurse came in to put the epidural in. I can't lie, I was shook when I saw that big ass needle. I managed to stop yelling at Trell for a minute so that he could hold my hand while they went through with the procedure. Once it started to kick in, I was able to mellow out a little. After a while, a nurse came in to do an ultrasound.

"Hello Miss McCray, I'm Nurse Brittany." she greeted. "I need to get a quick look, at your little girl."

"That's fine," I said.

I wasn't in pain anymore, but I was too uncomfortable to have a conversation with her. She hooked everything up, and put the gel on my stomach. She moved the probe around my stomach as she tried to find lil mama. I watched the screen as if I knew what she was looking for, but that thing was so confusing for me. You would think that after seeing at it for nine months, I'd be able to make out something on there. I tried to focus on the screen but I couldn't ignore the worried look on the nurse's face.

"Is everything okay?" I asked.

"Well, she seems to be turned the wrong way," she explained. "I'll go grab the doctor so he can take a look."

She left the room, and came back minutes later with my obstetrician, Dr. Johnson. He put more gel on my stomach and started moving the probe around.

"Yeah, I think we're gonna have to do a C-section." He said.

"I don't know about all that," I said. "Is that the only way we can get her out?"

"My fear is that if she tries to come out on her own, she could severely injure herself."

I squeezed Trell's hand. I've heard horror stories about women getting C-sections. I didn't want to put my body through surgery, but I wanted my baby here safely.

"Do whatever you have to do to get her here," I

said. "Can I be put to sleep?"

"We can do that. Give us some time to get you scheduled, and we'll send an anesthesiologist over."

"Thank you."

Dr. Johnson left the room with the nurse on his heels. Trell kissed me on my forehead and rubbed my stomach.

"Everything is gonna be okay, babe." He said.

"I know. I'm just nervous."

About forty five minutes later, Nurse Brittany came in to let me know that they were about to send the anesthesiologist over so that they could do the emergency C-section. Hearing the word emergency sent me into a bit of a panic Before I could freak out too much, there was a knock on the door. A petite older woman walked in the room with another machine.

"Hi I'm Jackie the anesthesiologist. I'm gonna give some medicine to help you go to sleep for your delivery."

She was trying to explain what she was doing as she was doing it, but once she stuck that damn tube down my throat, it was a wrap. I wish someone would've told me that shit had to happen in order for me to be put to sleep. If I'd known, I would've sucked it up and just had them numb me. After a while, I felt myself drifting off to sleep. As I closed my eyes, I said a prayer asking for everything for my daughter to make it here safely.

* * * * * * * * * *

I woke up feeling completely out of it, and my throat hurt like shit. I was expecting to see Trell in the room, but instead it was just Jackie and me.

"Where is my fiancé?" I asked.

"He went downstairs to bring some people up, he told me to let you know if he wasn't here when you woke up."

"Where is my baby?" I asked, franticly.

"She's right next to you, dear."

I was so out of it that I didn't realize that my daughter was in the bassinet by my bed.

"May I ask her name?" Jackie asked.

"Her name is Somaiya," I answered. "Somaiya Jacqueline Livingston."

Jackie admired my little girl for a few seconds, before shuffling out of the room. I looked at my baby girl sleeping, and then looked around the room. It seemed like yesterday, I was sitting in a similar room praying that her father survived being shot. Now not only was he alive, but we were ready to tackle this new world of parenthood together. I couldn't lie; the thought of being responsible for this little person scared the hell out of me. Trell would never admit it, but I knew that it scared him too. No one was around to show him what fatherhood was supposed to look like. He didn't have an Uncle Leon like I did, to act as a father figure. He had to learn how to be a man on his own. I knew he would be okay, but I know that he was worried about failing our daughter. I always told him that as long as he did right by her, he could never fail her. He was a good man, and I had no doubt in my mind that he would figure out fatherhood.

In the midst of my thinking, I heard someone open the door to my room. I turned around to see my mother peaking around the curtain. I could tell that she saw treading lightly, but I wanted her in here.

"Come on, it's okay." I said.

"I didn't want to wake ya'll up," She whispered.

"Somaiya is sleeping, and I just woke up. It's all good."

My mother stood over the crib and watched her sleeping granddaughter.

"She's beautiful," she said. "She looks just like her father."

"Yeah, I know. I guess it's true that your baby looks like the person who stressed you out the most during your pregnancy," I joked. "Where is her by the way.

"After he brought me up, he went to go find food," She said. "He said he hadn't eaten since last night."

"He was too busy making sure I was okay, lil mama had us worried."

An awkward silence filled the room. This was the first time in a while that we'd been by ourselves. I could tell that she didn't really know what to say, and I felt the same way. I wanted to squash everything, but I didn't know if it was the right time. One of us needed to say something, because it should never be like this with us.

"Taela, I'm sorry." She said, breaking the silence.

I didn't want to get emotional. Hell, I tried my hardest not to, but the fact of the matter was that I was in pain. The thing that was hurting me the most was that I couldn't even express how much pain I was in without revealing to her that I killed him. She, like most people, thought that he was on the run, and more than likely out of the country. Still she was very much aware of how I felt about him when I was younger, and she said nothing. I don't think that will ever sit well with me.

"Why would you let me hate my brother?" I asked.

She sighed, "I want to say that I was protecting you, but I was just being selfish."

"At least you're being honest now." I said.

"Do you think that was easy for me Tae?" she asked. "Every time I watched him run around the neighborhood, I wanted to say something."

"Still you thought it was better for you that I suffered. You know how bad I wanted to meet my siblings."

"What do you want me to say Tae?" She said with frustration. "I'm sorry I let my hatred for the boy's mama keep you from a relationship with him.

She paused and waited for me to say something, but I was all out of words. On one hand, it was something about her tone that didn't sit well with me. It just seemed like she was only apologizing because I was upset about it, not because she meant it. On the other hand, this was my mother. I knew she loved me, and even though she made a bad decision, I know her intentions were never to hurt me.

"Ma, I can't say that I understand where you're coming from, but I know that you love me and that's all that matters at the end of the day."

"I love you Taela," she said, kissing me on the forehead.

Before she could get another word in, there was another knock on the door.

"Come in!" I called out quietly.

"We're here!" Envy exclaimed very loudly.

I immediately checked on Somaiya, who flinched when she heard the noise.

"Envy, if you wake up my daughter I'm going to fight you."

"You threats won't work on me today Tae. The only thing I care about is our little girl."

Dani stepped in front of Envy.

"Move girl, let me see my niece." She said, as she picked Somaiya up.

"Ya'll are going to spoil her and she isn't even two days old." I said.

"Oh hush, that's what we're here for," Envy joked. "We spoil them and send them back."

"Technically, that is the grandmother's job," my

mother said, as she took the baby from Dani.

As crazy as they were, this was my family and I missed kicking it with them every day. Ever since Trell and I moved in together, Dani had been living with Jonathan so she'd been wrapped up in him. They seemed to be doing well, and he even mentioned to Trell a couple times that he was planning to propose at some point. I was happy for her, she was finally getting everything she wanted, and she deserved it. As in love as we were with our men, neither of us could touch the level of boo'd up Envy was on. She recently started dating a guy named Ramon, and they never left each other's side. I was actually surprised he didn't come to the hospital with her, because everywhere you saw her, you saw him. At first, it was hard to have girl talk with him always lurking around, but after a while, I didn't even notice him. I just hoped she wasn't moving too fast with him.

I tried to stay up and kick it with everyone, but the meds hadn't worn off completely and I dozed off. The last thing I remembered was my mother telling stories about her birthing experience. When I woke up, I was surprised to see that Dani was still there holding Somaiya. Trell, on the other hand, was in the recliner in the corner knocked out with his mouth open.

"Why are you still here?" I asked.

"I stayed so you could get some sleep," she said. "You passed out while we were playing with baby girl."

"Damn, I don't even remember falling asleep." I laughed. "I damn sure don't remember Trell coming in."

"Girl, he came in, saw that you were sleeping, and posted up in the chair."

"Well damn, did he at least feed her?"

"I took care of all that. You know I got ya'll."

The one thing I was happy about was that while we were in the hospital all the visitors wanted to change and feed her. I ate that up because I knew that once we got home that would be over.

Dani continued, "She's sleeping now, so I'm going to go so ya'll can get some family sleep time."

I laughed, "Thanks, D."

She walked Somaiya over too her crib, and kissed her forehead before gently putting her down.

"She's so pretty." She said, while stroking her hair.

I chuckled, "I still can't believe that we made a little human."

"Not too long ago, we were little humans."

We both laughed. Dani went quiet and stared at Somaiya. I knew that motherhood was something she's always wanted. Knowing what happened with her aborting King's baby back in the day, I was hoping that it wasn't upsetting her.

I said, "Your time is coming sooner than you know."

"I don't know about all that," she said. "I keep going back and forth. One day I want a baby, and the next I want to wait. I have a lot that I need to do first."

"I feel you on that. If I could go back, I would've waited. The club was just starting to take off-"

Dani cut me off, "No talking about work. Focus on your family."

"I'm sorry." I said, "I'm just saying, I would've waited if given a do-over."

"Well she's here now, and you're getting married soon. I'd say that everything is going as planned."

Dani kissed Somaiya one last time, and then kissed me on the cheek.

"Call me when you get home." I said.

"Will do," she replied before leaving.

After Dani left, I watched Trell sleeping. He had on some random sweats, mismatched socks with Nike slides, and his locs were thrown up in a messy bun. It was so unusual for him not to be kept up, but I knew that it was due to him being exhausted. With the way he was passed out on the chair, you would think he was the one who just went through major surgery. I couldn't blame him for being tired though. Especially after the hell he'd been through during my pregnancy. He'd been on the receiving end of all of my frustration, and I know he was sick of running to get me apple juice and putting up with my mood swings. He'd been amazing throughout this whole journey, and I would always love him for it.

## CHAPTER 2

I was more than happy when it was time for us to go home. I missed my bed, and I wanted a home cooked meal. My mom was going to stay with us for two weeks, so I knew that she would take care of the cooking for me. I could cook, but my mom could throw down. I was definitely looking forward to having her around for the next couple of weeks, especially now that we've made up.

When we pulled up to the house, I couldn't wait to go in and take a nap, but I knew Trell wasn't letting that happen. He was super over protective of both me and the baby, so I know he would want to be on my ass about everything the doctor said. For one, this fool actually bought a wheelchair for me so that I didn't have to walk from the car to the house. Then once we got inside he tried to carry my upstairs, not realizing that would hurt me more than walking. Luckily, I was able to convince him that I could do that on my own.

Once I got upstairs, I got semi undressed, and called Trell to help me into the bed. Of course he comes up behind me and tried to get something started. It's ironic that the same man who didn't want me walking upstairs on my own, wanted to have sex three days after I had a C-section.

"You have no clue how happy I am to be sleeping next to you again," he said as he kissed the back of my neck.

"If you don't chill your ass out," I said, pushing him away.

"What did I do?"

"Nothing yet, but I know what you're trying to do."

He ignored me, and started kissing on my neck again. I pushed him harder this time, and he flew backwards into the bedroom door.

"No Trell, and if you don't stop I'm gonna make you sleep in the guest room."

I hated to do it to him, but he would have to wait the six weeks just like I did. I didn't want him messing nothing up, and I didn't want to chance getting pregnant again so soon.

"Okay, I get it," he said, throwing his hands up. "Just know when those six weeks are up, I'm all over that ass."

He finished helping me get in the bed, and went back downstairs to get the rest of the bags. Along with our hospital bags, he brought my phone back with him. I must've left it in the car.

"Dani has been blowing you up," he said. "You should probably call her back before you go to sleep."

"Thank you," I replied.

Trell handed me my phone and went back downstairs to finish unloading the car. I called Dani back, and became irritated after the fourth ring. She always did this, and I wasn't in the mood to play phone tag with her today. Right before I was ready to hang up the phone, she picked up.

"Hey mama, how are you feeling?" she asked.

"I'm good, but I know that's not what you've been calling me for." I answered.

"You're right, but I wanted to check on you before I dropped this on you."

"What is it?" I asked, nervously.

The only thing I could think of was something being wrong with the club. Dani and Envy had been running things since my eighth month of pregnancy. I've said it before, and I'll say it again Tae's Place is my dream, and I'd lose it if something happened to it.

"Please tell me that nothing serious happened at the club," I continued.

"The club is fine, but some girl named Angie keeps coming her looking for you." She said.

"Just tell her I'm on maternity leave, and I'll get back to her in a few weeks."

Dani sighed, "She says she's your sister."

I almost dropped the phone when I heard the word sister. I knew that there were more Brooks children running around somewhere, but I never thought that they were ever out here looking for me. I honestly didn't know that any of them, other than King, knew who I was. Then again, this could be a lie. Either way, I needed to figure out what was going on.

"Tae are you still there?" Dani said, shaking me from my thoughts.

"Yeah, I'm here," I responded. "Just give her my number, and have her call me."

"Are you sure? I don't want it to be an issue if it doesn't have to be."

"No it's good. Just give her my number."

"Okay, I'll give it to her." Dani said before hanging up the phone.

I sat up on the bed, and stared at my phone. I hoped she called soon and didn't wait too long. I wouldn't be able to sleep with this weighing on my mind. Less than two minutes later, my phone rang and a Maryland number flashed across the screen. I took a deep breath, and answered it.

"Hello," I said. "Is this Angie?"

"Yes, this is she." She answered.

The line went silent. There was so much to say that neither one of us knew where to start. I had always talked about what I would do when I met one of my siblings, only to turn mute when it actually happens. Go figure!

"I wanted to see if we could meet up and talk." Angie said.

"I don't know," I replied. "How do I know that this is real?"

"Well, my mother was sleeping with our father while your mom was with him. Her name is Geniece. I'm sure if you asked your mother she'd remember her."

The thought of asking my mother to relive anything that happened with my father made me cringe. It was definitely a sore spot for her, and asking her about one of his sidepieces is something I didn't want to do. I'd have to get my information from Uncle Leon.

"I'm sorry Angie, but I need a little more than that to go off of."

"Jahrell and I met a month before he went on the run," She explained. "We took a DNA test."

The mere mention of King made me shiver. I wondered how much she knew about him.

"How did you find me?" I asked.

"I met our grandmother and I asked her about you," Angie said. "She told me to talk to Leon, but the streets told me that he relocated down here. When I came down here, I asked around and no one knew Leon, but they knew you because of your club."

"Look, that's cool and I but I need to think about it before I agree to see you. I just need to protect myself.

"I'll be in town for a few days, just call me if you want to talk."

I hung up the phone and stared at the floor, thinking about the conversation I just had. It was hard to grasp the fact that I could've possibly talked to my sister. It made me feel good to know that she was out there looking for me. I just needed to talk to Uncle Leon and my mother before I could sit with her. I didn't want to get too excited until I verified some things. I felt like Uncle Leon had to know something about the girl or her mother.

I turned over and tried to sleep but it wasn't happening, and when Trell came back into the room there was no way I was sleeping without telling him what just went down.

"Babe you won't believe what just happened." I said, startling him.

"First of all take your time sitting up, you might hurt yourself," he said. "Now, what happened?"

"Some woman named Angie has been coming to the club looking for me. She says she's my sister."

He sat down at the edge of the bed, and rubbed his temples. If anyone knew how much I was struggling with this, it was him.

"Did you talk to her?" He asked.

"Yup," I replied. "We spoke and she sounds legit. She said she and King took a DNA test."

The mention of his name put Trell on alert.

"You trust it?" He asked.

"I mean, the only thing I can do is meet her in person." I said, "I'm gonna call my uncle and see what he says first."

"That's probably the best thing to do at this point."

I started to call my uncle, but I wanted to pick my mother's brain about it first. So Trell helped me downstairs to the kitchen where I knew my mother would be. Surprisingly Uncle Leon was already here, so I could knock out two birds with one stone.

"Hey," I greeted. "When did you get here?"

"Don't mind me, why aren't you in bed?" he asked, as Trell helped me onto the couch.

"I need to talk to you and mom about something."

My mom looked concerned, "Is everything okay?"

"Essentially yes, but I got a phone call from a woman that says she's my sister."

My mother rolled her eyes, and Uncle Leon just looked confused. We all knew that my father had other kids out there, but I don't think either of us anticipated someone trying to get in contact with me.

"How do you know this is real?" My mom asked.

"She said that she took a DNA test with King before he went missing."

I made eye contact with my uncle who had been silent this whole time. I didn't know if he was processing, or if he just wanted to get all the facts before he said anything. I just needed him to say something. If anyone would know if this was true, it would be him.

"What do you think?" I asked him.

"I don't know what to think," he said. "We all know that Mike got around, but I can't say for sure that this is his daughter."

"Well, her name is Angie, and she said that her mother's name is Geniece."

"Oh wow," my mother said before going back into the kitchen.

Clearly, my mom knew who she was and I could tell by the look on my uncle's face that he knew too. My guess was that Geniece was someone that pops cheated on my mother with. As for Uncle Leon, I didn't know if he knew about Angie, or if he knew that Angie was my sister, but he definitely knew her mom.

"I think you should meet her," Uncle Leon suggested. "I'll go with you if you want."

"Well, I was thinking I would have her come here. I want my mother to be there too."

"I don't know about that, Tae. This could be a set-up, especially knowing that she's tight with King. I don't trust it fully."

"This is my house. She's outnumbered here," I said. "If she tries to crack slick, we'll get her out of here.

"If you

"If you're okay with it then set it up."

"Ma, is that cool with you?" I asked.

She was scrubbing g the counter vigorously. She only cleaned like that when she wanted to hide the fact that she was irritated by something. I completely understood why she would be, but I needed her support on this.

"I'm good with whatever you want Tae."

I quickly shot Angie a text asking her to come by. Surprisingly, hit me right back asking if she could come over in an hour. I sent her my address, and took a deep breath. The whole thing felt surreal. In about one hour, I would be meeting my sister.

I nervously played in my braids as I sat on my couch waiting for Angie to arrive. My mother tried to act as if she wasn't in her feelings, but I could tell she was. My uncle on the other hand was skeptical as usual. I knew that was because of him being in the streets for so long. He was taught to shoot first and ask questions later, so I appreciated him supporting me on this. The two of them being here, made up for Trell having leave out for work. While I was out on maternity leave, we needed all the money we could get so he didn't really have a choice. Plus, I'm sure he welcomed any break he could get from me fussing at him all day.

Around eight fifteen there was a knock on the door. My mother scurried over to let Angie in. I don't know what I was expecting her to look like exactly, but I was slightly surprised to see her in person. She was a little taller than Dani, caramel complexioned, and wore waist length faux locs. I didn't know how she was carrying the weight of them because she couldn't have been more than one fifty soaking wet. I was trying to see if she resembled my father, or King in any way but, I couldn't see it. My mother led Angie into the living room, where my uncle and I were sitting. She awkwardly waved at us, which made me feel better about how nervous I was.

"Hi I'm Tae," I said. "You can come in and have a seat. I apologize for not greeting you at the door, but I'm two days post-partum."

"I understand," she replied, as she sat down in between my mother and me.

There was an awkward silence between the three of us. Before it got too weird, Uncle Leon walked in the room with Somaiya, who was crying her eyes out. He went straight to the kitchen, grabbed a bottle out of the fridge, and plopped down next to my mother on the couch. I had to laugh because since we came home, he'd been more attached to her than her own grandmother. Once he got a look at Angie, he looked like he had seen a ghost.

"You look just like your mother," he said.

Angie immediately teared up.

"Thank you," she replied. "You still look the same as all of your pictures from back in the day. My mom used to show me pictures of you, my father, and my Uncle Ant."

"Aww man, Ant was that nigga back in the day," he reminisced. "Me, Ant, and Mike used to cause all types of trouble all over the place."

Angie laughed, "I've heard all about it. He was actually the person who told me how to find grandma."

"I'm not surprised. Mom has been living in the same place for years, and your uncle and mother were always over there –" he stopped mid-sentence. "It makes sense now."

"I'm so lost right now," I said.

"Your father and Geniece had an on and off fling for years. He told me he broke it off right before he moved in with Jacqueline, but I'm assuming Niecey must have already been pregnant."

My mother let out a disappointed chuckle, and stormed out of the room. I'm sure hearing that, added to the list of things my father lied to her about, but I would have to check on her later.

"Is she okay?" Angie asked. "I didn't mean to cause any trouble."

"She'll be fine," I said. "Uncle Leon, did daddy ever take a paternity test that you know of?"

"Hell no," he answered. "Mike said that Niecy was lying and kept it pushing. We all knew she was pregnant, but he said it wasn't his, and we believed him."

"If it helps, I have the results of the test I took with Jahrell."

"Can I see them?"

She pulled a large envelope out of her purse, and handed it to me. Sure enough, it was right there in black and white, she was our sister. I gave Uncle Leon the papers and he examined them, and gave them back to Angie.

"It's up to us how we want to move forward." He said.

"I mean, I want to get to know you all if it's not too much trouble." Angie said, "I don't mean to intrude, and I realize that I may be asking for a lot with you just having the baby."

"How long are you here?" I asked.

"Well, I didn't plan on finding you so fast, so I got an Air Bnb for the next month."

"What about work?"

"I run the PR team for the Washington Wizards," she said. "I left my assistant in charge while I'm away, and I'll be picking up some temp work with the Hornets."

I chuckled, "I guess being a boss runs in the family."

"I guess it does," she replied with a smile.

Angie reached over and gave me a hug. I couldn't help it, but the tears started to roll. This is everything I wished I would've had a chance to have with King. However, in a way it made me feel a little guilty. I would never tell her my secret, and I felt bad because she did have a relationship with him. After our embrace, I felt a little more at ease. This was going to take some time to get used to, but overall I was happy that I was finally going to have a relationship with one of my siblings.

## CHAPTER 3

Two weeks in to being a mom, I was a hot mess. I was up and moving, but I was exhausted, and I hadn't felt like myself since I gave birth. The smallest things upset me, and sometimes it was hard for me to hold Somaiya without crying. My mother was still here but she would be leaving in a few days. I didn't want to seem like I couldn't handle my household on my own, so I needed to get it together. Then on top of that, I was going to start working again to get ready for a huge event we have coming up.

The upside to all of the craziness was that I'd been talking to Angie just about every day. While the first meeting went well, I couldn't stop thinking about how close she was with King. I wanted to pick her brain and ask her about it, but I didn't know how to do that without being suspicious. Especially because I wasn't sure what he had said about me, or if he even mentioned me at all. Even thought she'd been cool so far, having her around was still a new concept I'd have to get used to.

One thing I couldn't get used to, was the screaming Somaiya was doing right now. We had to switch her to a new formula, and she needed a bottle ASAP. I sent Trell out thirty minutes ago to get it, and his ass hadn't come back yet, I was trying to give him the benefit of the doubt, because this was all new to him too, but I couldn't take much more of Somaiya's crying. If he didn't come back soon, I was going to have to go get it myself.

"Ma!" I called, with no response.

"MA!" I yelled louder.

My mom slowly shuffled into Somaiya's room, and I could tell that she was sleeping. I she could take a nap while my child was screaming bloody murder, I'll never know.

"What's wrong Tae?" She answered.

"Please take her so I can go to the store," I pleaded. "Trell has been gone for a half hour, and I need to get her formula."

"Taela, she has formula downstairs."

"No, she has the old formula downstairs. Dr. Johnson told us to give her a different kind because of her sensitive stomach."

"Well it's only been thirty minutes Tae, it's not like the store is down the street."

"I really don't need this from you," I shot back. "Are you going to take her for me, or am I going to have to take her to the store with me?"

My mom sucked her teeth.

"Fine Taela, I got her." She said, as she took Somaiya from me.

I quickly ran to my room and threw on some shoes so that I could hurry back. However, as soon I got to the key ring downstairs, Trell came through the door.

"Where the hell have you been?" I yelled.

"Whoa, what's wrong?" he asked. "Is lil mama okay?"

"While you were out bullshitting, our daughter has been screaming her head off because she's hungry."

"Bullshitting?" he said, agitated. "I was at the damn store."

"Well your daughter has been in here screaming her head off!" I yelled.

"Babe I get it, but I can only drive so fast."

I snatched the bag from him, and went to the kitchen to make the baby's bottle.

"Tae, do you need me to feed the baby?" he asked, walking towards me.

I threw an empty bottle at him.

"You don't understand what I'm dealing with! You get to go to work, and not worry about a damn thing," I yelled.

I felt crazy for screaming at him the way I was, but I couldn't help it. I had been so overwhelmed the past couple weeks, and it felt like I was doing everything on my own. As bad as it sounded, I couldn't wait to go back to work, so I could have some type of break.

Trell picked up the bottle I threw, and walked over to me.

"Go lay down for a little bit. I'll feed lil mama and put her to bed. Then I'll come check on you."

He tried to hug me, but I side stepped him and went up to our room. My mother had somehow gotten Somaiya to quiet down, and I was happy because the noise was starting to get to me. I was trying to keep it together but I felt so weighed down by everything going on. I was still having mixed feelings about everything, especially motherhood. In an attempt to reclaim my peace of mind, I laid in my bed and pulled the covers over my head. Shortly after, I felt movement on my bed, so I popped up from under the covers to see what it was. I rolled my eyes when I saw Trell, sitting at the edge of the bed undressing. I wasn't surprised that he followed me up here, but I just wanted him to leave me alone. It seemed like I could never get a free moment to myself, and I really needed it.

"Can you sleep downstairs please?" I asked.

He sighed, "Are you really that mad at me?"

"Can you just leave me alone and go downstairs?"

"Tae, I want to sleep in my bed tonight," he said. "I'm tired, I've been working all day, and I just want to sleep next to my woman."

"I don't care what you want. I need you to go downstairs."

"Tae I get that you're upset because I took too long, but it's not that bad that I should have to sleep in another room."

I picked up my phone and beamed it at him. It hit the mirror on our dresser, and glass fell to the floor.

I screamed, "Get the fuck out Trell!"

Somaiya started to cry. Trell started to go get her but I stopped him before he could.

"Don't touch my daughter!" I yelled.

Before Trell could get a work out, Uncle Leon came running in the room. He looked like he was ready to fuck Trell up, and in this moment I'd let him. I just wanted him to leave me alone and stop stressing me out.

"Trell, step out and take a drive so things can calm down," Uncle Leon said. "Somaiya doesn't need the negative energy around her, and Tae you need sleep."

Trell shook his head, and stormed out of the room. I thought he was going to the living room until I heard the front door slam.

"Am I supposed to be okay with him leaving like that?" I asked.

"Tae, he's coming back. You need to go to sleep, and I'll look after little mama."

I sighed, "Whatever."

If this were anyone else, I would've argued them down, but it wasn't worth it. If Uncle Leon says 'go to bed', that's exactly what I was going to do.

Waking up alone the next morning felt all too familiar. Then again, I couldn't be too upset with him for staying out all night. There was a slight possibility that I overreacted about the formula, but I honestly couldn't help it. I felt so out of control with the baby throwing a fit, and I just reacted. All I could think about as I showered was what happened last time I was in this situation. I promised myself that no matter what, I wouldn't go down that road again.

After getting dressed, I went downstairs to make Somaiya a bottle before she woke up. When I got to the living room, I was happy to see Trell sleeping on the couch, but I was thrown off by the strong odor he was emitting. He smelled like a damn frat house. I shook my head and continued into the kitchen to make the bottle.

"What the hell is that smell?" my mother asked, as she came around the corner.

"Apparently Trell bathed in a bar last night." I said.

"Just let him sleep it off, and ya'll can talk about last night later."

"I don't think we have anything to talk about."

"Taela, you chewed that man out for taking thirty minutes to go to the store," She said. "By the way, thirty minutes is quick considering how far it is."

"Of course you take his side." I retorted.

"It isn't about sides. You did entirely too much last night, and I'm worried about you."

I laughed, "You're acting like I beat him up!"

"You whooped his ass verbally, and he was just trying to be a good father. This is new to him too!"

"I'm done talking about this."

I finished making the bottle, and left the kitchen.

"You can run from it all you want Tae, but you need to talk to someone."

"Did we not just talk?" I said turning around.

"No, I mean professionally. It seems like you're dealing with postpartum depression."

"I'm fine ma. I'm not depressed." I said, "I was just a little frustrated with lil mama crying. She's good now, so I'm good."

"Whatever you say, Taela. I just want you to be okay."

She was making something out of nothing. I wasn't depressed, or even sad for that matter. Life was great for me right now. I was just a tad bit overwhelmed with being a new mother, but I'd get over it eventually.

On my way through the living room, I heard Trell's phone ringing. I went to see who it was, and saw the name Aylin flash across the screen. I'd never heard that name before, so I assumed it was one of his employees.

"Trell, wake up. Aylin is calling you."

He quickly shot up, as if I scared him. He grabbed the phone from me, ignored the call, and went back to sleep. Whoever it was, called back immediately. This time, I answered.

"Hello," I greeted.

As soon as I spoked, the line went dead. I wasn't sure of who was on the other line, but it didn't sit well with me. I let it go for the time being, but I would definitely be bringing this back up once he was sober.

I went to Somaiya's room to give her the bottle. I watched her as she ate, and looking at her made me smile. My baby girl was now starting to look like me, and I loved it. I could tell by the color on her ears she would be closer to his chocolate brown complexion, but she had many of my facial features especially my lips. I couldn't wait for her personality to start developing. I hoped that she wouldn't get my stubbornness, although if she did I'm sure my mother would see it as karma.

I heard footsteps stop at the door, and saw Trell standing in the doorway. He looked horrible, and I still couldn't get past the smell.

"Please take a shower before you come in here." I

said.

"I just want to talk to you for a second."

I sighed, "You got five minutes."

"I'm sorry about last night. I know that I haven't been around a lot, and you need a break." He said, "I need to be more considerate in making sure you get some time to yourself."

I wouldn't let him see it, but he got to me. The revelation he just had was all I ever wanted from him. I just hated that we had to have an argument that, big to get him to be more attentive to his family.

"Trell I appreciate it. I know I acted a little crazy, and I apologize."

He leaned over to give me a hug and kiss. I wanted to act as if it didn't mean much, but truthfully, it meant everything. He had a way of putting me at ease and making everything be still for a moment, and I loved that about him.

"I love you Tae," he said. "I can't wait for the day I get to call you my wife."

I chuckled, "You're the one playing games with setting a date. I been told you that I'm ready."

He looked down at the floor.

"What's wrong?" I asked.

"Thinking about the wedding reminds me that Boo won't be here. I'm still trying to cope with it."

He hadn't brought up Boo in a while, so honestly I thought that he was okay with everything. With everything going on, it never occurred to me to check on him and see how he was doing.

"Babe it's really no rush. I need to heal up anyway. We can revisit this in a few months."

He leaned over and kissed me again, "Thanks babe."

"Now please take a shower," I said. "I don't want your strong ass odor upsetting my baby."

Trell shot me the middle finger and laughed before going to the bathroom. I was happy the conversation went the way it did. There was still the matter of that phone call he got earlier, but it honestly wasn't important right now. We were good, and I wanted it to stay that way.

# CHAPTER 4

Things calmed down around the house, and I was finally starting to feel like I was getting my life in order. I had finally worked Somaiya into a routine that worked for the both of us, and she was starting to cry a lot less. I was extremely happy that everything was coming together since my mom was leaving in a few days. She was supposed to leave last week, but after the blow up with Trell and I, she stayed a little longer to make sure that I was okay. I kept telling her that I was fine, but she wasn't hearing it. She had a crazy idea about me being the depressed, but that was far from the case.

Despite the minor hiccup I'd had, I was very happy with my family in all aspects. I was good with my fiancé, I was speaking to my mother and uncle again, and I was starting to form a relationship with my sister.

Angie had only come around once since we first met up, but we still spoke every day. We made plans to meet up for breakfast since Trell took off today. I was excited to finally spend some time with her without having to get up and check on the baby, or being mindful of our conversation so that my mother didn't get in her feelings. Even though she knew my father had an issue with fidelity; it still hurt her to have a reminder of cheating hanging around. She never said anything directly, and she was always nice to Angie, but I could tell that she wasn't happy about having her around.

I got out of bed, and went to check on the Somaiya. I couldn't help but to smile when I saw that Trell had already made his way in to feed her. He was staring deeply in her eyes, and he didn't have to say a word for me to know what he was thing, because I did the same thinking. It was still so surreal to me that we created a beautiful little person. Moments like these put our household in such a peaceful place. It had been a little over a week since I spazzed out on Trell, and he had done a great job making sure I got some kind of break from Somaiya, which was needed.

"She's so pretty." I said, as I walked over to them.

"Just like her mama," he answered, looking up at me.

"Yeah right," I said, chuckling. "I'm glad she's finally starting to look like me."

"Yeah, well she definitely eats like you," he said, holding up the empty bottle. "She destroyed this bottle."

"Shut up," I said, playfully slapping him on the back of the head.

Trell gently laid Somaiya in her crib, and came to give me a kiss.

"What do you have planned for the day?" he asked.

"Well, Angie and I are going go to breakfast and maybe do a little shopping afterwards."

"How are you feeling about her?"

"She's great; it feels like I've known her my whole life."

"That's wassup, just be cautious with her."

I sighed, "What are you getting at La' Trell."

"All I'm saying is that she had a relationship with your bitch ass brother," He explained. "You need to keep an eye on her."

"She barely knew him."

"But she did know him." He replied, "You don't know what he told her, and you don't know what the streets back home are saying. This could all be a set up."

I was annoyed. I couldn't figure out if it was because I felt like he was being insensitive, of if it was the fact that he could be right. I was so happy to meet my sister that I hadn't taken the time to think about this realistically.

Trell noticed that he may have struck a nerve, and hugged me from behind.

"Just be careful," he said, as he softly kissed my neck. "Your daughter and I need you. I don't know what I would do if someone took you away from us."

"I know you're just looking out babe, but I got this." I said, trying to end the conversation.

"Yeah, but I'm still gonna lookout for you."

I turned around and hugged him tightly before giving him a kiss.

"I need to get ready to go," I said. "Angie is picking me up in an hour."

"Okay, I'm gonna get myself something to eat." He replied, "Watching lil mama tear that bottle up made me hungry as hell."

I laughed before going back to my room to go get ready. I took a quick shower, and put on some foundation. I cringed when I got a look at my hair. These braids had definitely see better days, and I needed to take them out ASAP. I got them done right before my due date because I knew I wouldn't have time to bother once Somaiya came, but now I was over them. Nonetheless, I put them in a messy bun, and went to the closet to put on some jeans and my black Tae's Place T-shirt. Just because I wasn't working, didn't mean I couldn't advertise. I slipped on a pair of black white and gold air maxes, and headed downstairs to wait for my ride.

To my surprise, Angie was already in my kitchen waiting for me. She was talking to Trell as he was making his favorite breakfast of eggs, turkey bacon, and French toast. I loved that despite his reservation, they seemed to be getting along. That was one less issue for me to worry about.

"Hey sis," I greeted.

"Hey, you look cute," Angie said as she gave me a hug. "I was just in here trying to get my brother in law to hook a sister up with some sneakers."

Trell jumped in, "I told her if she can get me some

floor seats for the Hornet's and Warriors game, I'll let her get two pairs."

"You know I'm good for it. It's still in the preseason, so it'll be easy for me to work my magic." She replied.

"Well, I'm down for an even trade. Work your magic, and I'll work mine."

I checked the time on my phone, and we needed to leave before Ihop got busy.

"As much as I love to see ya'll getting alone, Angie and I need to go so we won't have to wait forty five minutes for a table."

"True." Angie said.

I gave Trell a kiss goodbye, and we were on our way. Luckily, we only had to wait about ten minutes to be seated at the restaurant. I couldn't figure out why, but for some reason at this particular Ihop, if you didn't get in by ten in the morning, you were sure to wait at least forty-five minutes for a table. When we arrived, it wasn't empty, but it also hadn't hit the breakfast rush yet. Once we were seated, the waitress came and took our drink orders, and left Angie and me to our conversation.

"So, how have things been going with lil mama?"

Angie asked.

"We've finally got her on a routine, and she's been doing better with the crying." I replied, "I'm glad because I don't know how I would've functioned if we didn't calm that down.

Angie laughed, "You would've managed. After a while, you learn to tune it out. My first job was working at a daycare, so I've mastered the art of tuning children out."

"Do you want kids?"

"Ehh, I don't know. I'm always on the move, and that type of lifestyle doesn't really leave room for a family."

I chuckled, "It's genetic, daddy used to be the same way. I'll have Uncle Leon to tell you stories about when they were kids."

Angie gave a dry laugh.

"What was he like?" she asked, somberly.

"Well, I only have vague memories because I was only five when he passed," I said. "I do remember him being loving and playful with me."

"Jahrell said the same thing," she responded. "Were you two close?"

"Nah, we weren't. We've known each other for a

long time, but we didn't know we were related."

"He told me that you two went to school together, and that he was friends with Trell."

I looked up confused, and on guard. I guess this is why everyone kept saying that I needed to see what her relationship with King was. I didn't know why he would say something like that to her. I guess it was his way of fucking with me in the afterlife.

"Did he really?" I asked suspiciously.

"Yes, he said that he and your fiancé were close."

I laughed, "He meant my former fiancé, Shaun. He passed away about a year ago."

"I'm so sorry," she said, embarrassed.

"It's okay, you didn't know." I replied. "Besides, there was a lot of good that came from it. I moved down here, opened my club, and met the love of my life. I'm good.

"You have done well for yourself down here. How does it feel to be off work?"

"It's been a struggle. I don't feel like myself."

"Why not?" She asked.

"I'm grateful for Lil mama, but I feel like my life isn't mine anymore."

It felt crazy to say aloud, and I felt like I wasn't

making any sense. I just knew that since the baby, I haven't felt right. I was either cussing someone out, or crying uncontrollably. I hated to feel like I was saying that Somaiya was the reason for it, but I never felt like this before.

"Is there something going on at the club that you can work on from home?" she questioned. "That may help with the transition."

"There's a charity event with the Hornets next month, but it would be hard to run it from home."

"Why don't you talk to Trell about going back to work?" she asked. "Just go back for the charity event."

"I don't think he would go for it. He was already trippin about me having a nanny when I go back to work full time."

"All you can do is ask right?"

The more I thought about it, the more I knew she was right. The most he could say was no, and then I'd just go do it anyway. I knew I would lose my mind if I didn't figure out something soon. I needed to feel like myself again, and this was the only way I knew how.

After my breakfast date with Angie, I came home to Trell and my uncle kickin' it in my living room. I didn't see Lil' Mama with them, so she was probably in her

room or with my mom. I was supposed to talk to Trell
about going back to work, but since he was bonding
with my uncle, I decided that it would have to wait
until later. So I continued with the rest of my day,
trying to figure out how I was going to have the
conversation. At the end of the day, I decided that the
only way to do was to put it all out there. I knew that
he wouldn't be happy with it, but it was what I wanted
so he would respect it. When he was giving Somaiya
her nighttime feeding, I came into her room and sat on
the bed next to her crib.

"Hey babe, I need to talk to you about something,"
I said nervously.

"Is everything okay?" he asked.

"Everything is fine, but I wanted to see how you felt
about me going back to work for a few days."

"I thought ya girls had everything covered?" he
asked.

"They do, but I wanted to work on the Hornets'
fundraiser."

"I don't like it." He said, "Who's gonna be here with
the baby?"

"Well, my mom will be here, and I was gonna see if
the nanny could start working early."

Trell shook his head, I knew that he didn't want to agree to it, but he knew that he had no choice. Once I had my mind set on something, you couldn't tell me no.

"Fine, Taela." He said, "Only for the fundraiser, and then you need to come home and finish your leave."

"Thanks, babe." I replied.

I hopped up off the bed cheerfully, and kissed him on the cheeked. I ran back in to our room to get myself ready for work.

The next morning, I was happy to be finally getting back to work. Although it was brief, I was happy to be back in my club. This party was for a very important client, and if it went well, it would be amazing advertisement. Today I would just be meeting with Dani and Envy to divide the tasks. I was happy to see the ladies, especially Envy. Dani had been by the house plenty of times to see Somaiya, but I hadn't seen Envy since they came to the hospital. I wasn't upset about it, I was sure she was busy with her new man, and I completely understood.

Walking in and seeing her behind the bar balancing the cash register made me smile. She'd come so far from being our bottle girl, and I loved seeing her evolve.

"Hey Miss Manager," I greeted.

"Hey boss lady!" She exclaimed. "We've really missed you around here."

"I've missed ya'll too. I'm glad to see everything is running well."

"You know Dani and I weren't going to let anything happen to this place."

"Speaking of Dani, is she here? I didn't see her car."

"She's been driving Jonathan's car, so it wouldn't be out there. She's in your office waiting for you. I'll be back there once I finish with this drawer.

I went back to my office to find Dani sitting at the conference table. Last, I saw her she had a long weave, and now she was sporting at dark red short cut. I loved when she wore her shorts cuts, but she changed her hair so much they never stayed for very long. Either way she looked good, and I was here for every minute of it.

"Hey boo, how are you?" she asked.

"I'm good, I'm just happy to be back even if it is for a little bit."

"Yeah right, I already know how this is gonna go," she replied. "You're gonna love it too much, and talk Trell into staying past the event."

We both laughed.

"Let's see how this goes first," I said. "I may finish with the party and decide that it's too much. Besides, ya'll have been holding it down here."

"You know I have. We've had some minor issues with staff, but you know I'm not taking their shit."

"Let me guess; the bottle girls?"

Dani rolled her eyes, "Of course. They're fighting over customers, tips, uniforms, and anything else they can think of to piss me off."

"Oh gosh, do you need me to come in and get them together?"

"Nope, I told them if we have one more incident I'm getting rid of people."

"Well, it seems like you got it under control. Just let me know if you need anything."

Just as we finished our conversation, Envy popped in.

"Sorry to make ya'll wait." She apologized.

"It's no problem." I replied, "This shouldn't take long. I just wanted to talk about what needs to be done for the Hornet's fundraiser."

"How many people are they expecting?" Dani asked.

"They're saying two to three hundred." I replied, "That's only in attendees. I'm leaving an allowance for up to fifty staff members so that we don't have any issues with the fire marshal."

"Yeah, you know how they like to trip." Envy added.

"Do you think we're going to need fifty staff members?" Dani asked.

"No but I like to overestimate," I explained. "Is that not a good number?"

"I guess it's fine." She replied.

I gave Dani a slight side eye and continued speaking.

"There are a few things that need to be done in the upcoming weeks and I figured that we'd split them."

"Okay, what are they?" Envy asked.

"First of all, we're about twenty people short as far as staff, so we'll need to hire some temps. Dani can you do that?"

"I think it would be good for Envy to get staffing experience." She replied.

"That's true," I agreed. "Envy can you handle that?"

"I sure can." She said,

"Well Dani you can link with the planner and get catering figured out."

"I also think it would be good experience for Envy to have." She replied.

I looked up from my computer, "Dani you created the menu, and you have a better rapport with the chefs. It would be best for you to take this one."

"You and I both created the menu," she shot back.

"I gave some input here and there, but that was all you. What's the issue?"

"Well, if we're trying to fully train Envy to be a manager, I think she should play a huge part in this party so that people can see her face more."

"It's cool Tae, I can do it," Envy chimed in.

"Dani she is going to have plenty to do during the process, it just makes sense for you to deal with the catering."

Dani rolled her eyes, "Whatever Tae, I got it."

I didn't know what was going on, but clearly, something was wrong. Dani had a way of being passive aggressive when something was bothering her, instead of just saying what hell the problem was. With everything going on at home, the last thing I needed was tension between Dani and I.

"Envy, can we have the room?" I asked.

"Ya'll sure can," She responded.

Envy quickly left the room, and closed the door behind her.

"What's the problem, Dani?" I asked, "Why are you fighting me?"

She sighed, "All I'm saying is that we need to start getting Envy ready to take over my role."

"I thought that's what we were doing," I replied.

"I mean that we should start making the transition sooner rather than later."

"You're leaving?"

"When you come back full time I'm going to start looking for spaces to open up a shop."

"So this is the heads up I get?"

"Yeah I guess it is."

"I mean I knew this was going to happen eventually, but last we talked you made seem like it was a long way off."

"Well, since you've been gone I've realized that this is not where I belong. This isn't my club, it's yours, and I'm ready to do my own thing."

The tone of this conversation wasn't sitting well with me. Dani was coming off as if she had some sort of problem with me, and I've been gone for almost two months now. I was aware that I could be a lot to deal with at times, but it was never intentional.

"Dani, are we okay? It seems like you're upset with me."

"Tae you've been gone for a month now, and you come back in shouting out orders like I haven't been running this place."

"I know you have, and I've acknowledged that you've been doing a bomb ass job keeping this together, but at the end of the day this is 'Tae's place'. If this shit doesn't go right, it's my name of line not yours."

Dani scoffed, "I should've stayed my ass in Maryland."

"I didn't ask you to come here; you invited yourself!"

"I came because I knew that you needed me!"

"That's a different story than the one you gave back home. I guess all that talk about needing me was a crock of shit."

"Let's be real, you needed me down here with you."

"I would've figured it out."

"Like you figured Shaun out?" she shot back.

I was speechless. Dani was the last person I thought would throw some shit in my face, and it hurt like shit.

"You know what D, me and Envy got the event. Just train her on your club duties so you can be on your way out," I said. "I'm also coming back to work early. I don't trust you to run things the way the need to be ran."

"Girl bye," Dani replied sarcastically.

I gathered my things, and stormed out of my office.

"Is everything okay Tae," Envy asked when I walked past her.

"Hell no," I replied without stopping.

I hated fighting with Dani, and I wasn't pleased with how everything went down. Still, we had an event to prepare for and Envy had a lot to learn before she took over for as manager. I knew that Trell was going to throw a fit when I told him that I would be going back to work permanently, but he would get over it. I put a lot of work in to building my club, and I wasn't going to let it go to shit just because Dani was jumping ship. I'd die before I let that happen.

## CHAPTER 5

I decided to let things cool down between Dani and me before going back into the club. I thought she would've called me the night of our argument to give her apologies but she didn't. I don't think it would've done much for me anyways. I felt so betrayed by her, and it would take more than an apology to fix that. Not only was she abandoning me with Tae's Place, she went extremely low by bringing up Shaun. I'd packed all that shit away in the back of my mind, and the mere mention of his name brought back so many thoughts and feelings that I wanted to forget.

Since I wasn't physically going into the club to work, I'd been working in my home office like crazy. I put a bassinet for Somaiya in there and tried get some things done, but she was being extra needy today. Anytime I got in my groove of working, she'd start crying. Luckily, Angie was on her way to visit. Some time with her Auntie would be a perfect distraction for Somaiya, and would give me some time to make a couple of important phone calls. I tried to send out some emails before I got fed up and decided to wait for Angie come.

I took Somaiya with me to the living room so I could watch some TV. It was about time for Divorce Court to come on, and it had become such a guilty pleasure for me since I'd been on leave. Watching some of the couples gave me hope that Trell and I would be okay. Our issues were minor compared to the problems a lot of them were having. About halfway through the episode, there was a knock on the door. I felt a sense of relief. As much as I loved the show, I had work that I needed to do. Now that Angie was here, I could get some work done.

"Hey girl," I said after letting my sister in.

"Hey, I was surprised you were home," she said. "I thought you were working at the club."

"I am working; I'm just going to work from here. Dani and I got into an argument the other day."

"What was it about?"

"She doesn't like being second in command," I

explained. "She's used to being on her own, and she wants to open up a hair salon like the one she had back home."

"What's the problem with that?"

"It's not the fact that she wants to leave the club, it's just the timing. I'm out on maternity leave, and she decides to tell me now."

"So how are ya'll going to work together until she leaves?" Angie asked.

"For one, I'm going back to work permanently. Two, I'm just going to work from home until we're done with the event."

"Oh hell no," she exclaimed. "That's your club, you're going back tomorrow."

"I don't think it's a good idea."

"Nope, I'm not hearing it. We're going tomorrow."

"Where are ya'll going tomorrow?" Trell asked as he walked in the living room.

I'd been so wrapped up in conversation with Angie, I didn't hear him come through the door. We hadn't discussed my fulltime return to the club yet, and this wasn't how I wanted to tell him. I was also confused as to why he was home so early.

I sighed, "Well, we're going–"

"We're going to work at the club tomorrow," Angie interjected. "She's not going work from here like she's scared. She needs to let everyone know that she's back and here to stay."

I knew she was trying to help, but she wasn't. I hadn't told Trell any of this because I knew he would have a fit and tell me to finish out my leave. Sure, I was grown and at the end of the day, it was my decision. However since it would involve the baby, I still needed to talk it over with him.

"Oh word, when was this decided?" he asked.

Once Angie realized she let the cat out the bag, she quickly picked up Somaiya.

"I'm going to take Lil' Mama to her room so we can have some Auntie and me time," she said before speed waking to the baby's room.

"So you're back at work for good?" Trell asked.

"Not officially, but I am going back tomorrow."

"Wow, so you just decided this all without speaking to me about it?"

"You said it was cool!" I argued.

"I said it was cool for you to work one event," he said. "We never talked about fully ending your leave early."

"Trell, I should've told you about me going back to work and the argument with Dani, but-"

"Tae, I don't care about Dani or any argument!" he said. "I honestly don't care about you going back to work. You were about to make a huge decision that involves our child, and you didn't tell me."

"Trell, I was going to tell you when you got home today. You just happened to get here earlier than expected."

"I'm sure you were Tae. It's cool, go hang out with your sister. We'll finish this later."

Trell walked away from me and to the kitchen to sit at the island. Due to us arguing as soon as he got in, I didn't get a good temperature read on him. He was visibly stressed and I know I couldn't just be from me going back to work.

"Are you okay, babe?" I asked as I rubbed his back. "Why are you home so early?"

"It's been a rough day. I wasn't in the mood to deal with people today, so I came home."

"Do you want to talk about it?"

"No I don't really." He replied. "As a matter of fact, go ahead with your sister to the club. I got baby girl."

"Are you sure?"

"Yeah, I got her."

I went to Somaiya's room to get Angie. I was happy that she was going to be coming with me. Not only did I want her to see my hard work, but also I didn't want to be in the club with Dani by myself. I wasn't ready for that awkwardness.

When we arrived at the club, I was a little relieved to see that Dani's car wasn't there. She must've been running errands, which was great for me because I wouldn't have to see her. I was a little irritated when I got in because it seemed like a lot of the tasks that should have been done the night before weren't done. No one picked up the ice buckets from the VIP sections, and the first floor cash register hadn't been audited, meaning the money hadn't been deposited. All I could do was shake my head.

"What's wrong?" Angie asked.

I scoffed, "Dani wants to pop shit about me giving orders, but the basic shit isn't even done."

"Well, I'm here to help if you need me."

"Cool, come with me behind the bar. I'm going to count the drawer and place the money in stacks. I need you to recount and bind the stacks."

"It sounds easy enough."

We went around the bar and started counting the drawer; we got about halfway through before I heard keys in the front door. I was desperately hoping Envy walked through the door, but unfortunately, it was Dani.

"Hey, what are you doing here?" Dani asked. "I didn't think you be here for a few days."

"I've ended my leave early. I'm just auditing the drawer, which should've been done last night."

Dani chuckled, "I see you're still on bullshit, so I'm going to go to my office."

"Of course, we can talk about me all day, but the minute I speak on your unprofessionalism you run to your office." I called out after her.

Clearly, I struck a nerve, because she quickly hit a U-turn and came back to the bar.

"Tae, you can't speak to me about being unprofessional, when you have a stranger behind the bar counting money."

"Don't talk about my sister that way. She's helping me do what you didn't do last night."

"Be smart Tae, you just met her and she has last night's profits in her hand."

"Please don't speak about me like I'm not standing

right here," Angie said, jumping in.

"Bitch don't talk to me!" Dani shot back.

Knowing where this had the potential to go, I turned around and signaled for Angie to be quiet. I knew that she was sticking up for herself, but the last thing I needed was the woman who grew up with me like a sister, and my actual sister fighting.

"That's my sister and you're on your way out, so don't worry about what I'm doing." I said to Dani.

"You got it Taela, and since you're back you can run the club tonight," she said before going back to her office.

"Damn, is she always like that?" Angie asked.

"She didn't used to be, but we've been on rocky terms recently."

"I couldn't work like that every day."

"That's why I try to work from home." I said, "I can't even worry about that right now. We need to straighten up in here."

After balancing the drawer, Angie and I finished cleaning up the mess from the night before. The whole time we were cleaning, I was thinking of all the ways I was going to lay out my entire staff when they came in. Whether Dani enforced it or not, they knew damn well that they should leave the club a mess like this. It would've never gone down like this if I had been here. It was cool though, because I was back now.

After cleaning up the club area and the VIP booths, Angie and I started wiping everything down. As I wiped down the bar, the staff started to come in. I missed all of them, and I could tell by their reactions that the feeling was mutual. I got the biggest reaction when my head of security, Kylan, came in. He made it a point to call and check on me frequently since I'd been out, so to finally see him felt great.

"Ky! What's up?" I greeted enthusiastically.

Ky came around the bar and gave me a huge hug.

"Boss lady, I'm glad to see you back." He said. "I thought you wouldn't be back for a few more weeks."

"I wasn't, but the plan changed." I replied.

"Well, I'm not mad about it at all."

"How has everything been around here?" I asked.

"Operations wise everything has been fine, but there is a bit of an issue with the security team."

I could tell by the tone of his voice that this was a private conversation. So I led him to my office and shut the door.

I sighed, "What's going on Ky?"

"It's Gino," he said. "He's missing."

"Since when?"

"I haven't seen him since we left last night. Today the security team had a training and he was a no show."

"That's not like him at all," I said, "Have you called him?"

"I've called at least ten times with no answer. I feel like something isn't right."

The look on Ky's face had me shook. This is the first time since he'd been working for me that I saw fear in his eyes. He and Gino were close and I knew that he was worried about his friend.

"The only thing I can think of is to take a ride over there. If we leave now, we can make it back before the doors open."

"You don't have to come with me, I can go on my own."

"There's no way I'm letting you go by yourself. If some bullshit is going down, I don't wanna lose you too. Pull your car up and I'll meet you outside."

Ky shook his head, "You got it boss."

Once Kylan was gone, I opened my office safe, grabbed my gun, and put it in my purse. I hadn't carried it in a while, but I had no clue what I was walking into so I needed to be safe. On my way out the door, I spotted Envy talking to one of the bottle girls.

"E, I'm going to take a ride with Kylan. Hold down the fort." I said.

"Where's Danita?" she asked.

"She's in the back, but she's leaving soon. I'll explain when I come back," I explained. "Angie, I'll call an uber to take you to my house."

"Is everything okay," she asked.

"Yes, I just need to run somewhere and I don't want to leave you here alone."

"Okay, cool. I'll call you later."

I gave Angie a hug, and hurried out the door to catch up with Ky. When I got outside, he was sitting his black Denali. Once we pulled off, I looked around and admired the interior. I'd always loved these trucks, but I was way too short to drive one. I made a mental note to try to convince Trell to get one for our family car.

"I really wish you would've stayed back at the club," Ky said, bringing me back to the situation at hand.

"Listen, you know the whole staff is like family to

me. If something is wrong with one of ya'll I need to know," I replied. "Is G still running the streets?"

"Nah," he said. "I'd been keeping him busy with some freelance security work."

"Did he have any beef with any one?"

"What are you getting at, Ms. Taela?"

"I don't mean to insinuate anything, but I don't want to rule anything out."

"G was finally on the right path. There were a lot of times he wanted to go back to that lifestyle, but I wouldn't let him."

Ky's voice started to trail off. I could tell that this was a sore spot for him. I knew that Gino had a background of running the streets, but I had no clue that Ky was so instrumental in getting him out of it. I prayed that nothing terrible happened to him, because Ky would fall apart. After about fifteen minutes, the truck came to a stop.

"That's his spot over there," Ky said, pointing to a house on the left of us. "Should we try calling again?"

"Nah, let's just go knock on the door."

As we walked up the walkway to the house, I got a glimpse around back. I saw Gino's car parked on the parking pad, and it looked like someone was in it.

"Ky, G is back there sitting in the car. I told you he's alright."

I started walking over to the car, but Ky grabbed my arm to stop me.

"Let me go first." He instructed.

Ky walked in front of me and pulled out his gun. As we got closer, I could tell that he was right to be nervous about it. There was blood dripping from the driver's side, and when Ky opened the door we saw the reason why. Gino had been stabbed to death. It was one thing to see the dead body of your enemy, but to see someone you care about like that, it made me want to vomit. I knew I had no place being disturbed by it, but I was.

"Take my truck and my piece back to the club," Ky said. "You don't need to be anywhere near this."

"I'm not leaving you. I don't want them to think you did it."

"Get out of here, Tae!"

I did as I was told, and took Ky's truck back to the club. The whole ride I kept thinking about Gino going out like that. I was also worried about Ky because of how close they were. It was hard for me to imagine losing one of my closest friend like that. Even though

Dani and I were in our feelings on some petty shit, she was still my family and I needed to call her. I called her, and prayed that she picked up.

"What Tae?" she answered.

"D, I was calling to let you know that Gino was killed." I said through tears.

The line went quiet. I knew how Dani was; she needed a moment to process.

"What happened?" she asked, Did the police call you?"

"Me and Ky went to check on him, and we found him," I explained. "He was stabbed to death"

"Are you okay?"

"No, no I'm not. I just want to go home to my family."

This took a lot out of me, and I wanted nothing more than to hug my fiancé and daughter. I couldn't wait to get back to my car so I could get home to them.

"Go home, and I'll go back to the club."

"Are you sure?"

"Just because you're acting an ass, doesn't mean I don't have your back."

I chuckled, "I love you D.:

"I love you too T."

I hung up the phone and hurried back to the club to get my car. On the ride home, I tried to figure out how I was going to tell the rest of my staff about G. This was something that I never thought I was have to do as an employer. I decided to ask Trell to get his ideas about it, because I needed help. When I pulled up to my house, I was surprised to see Uncle Leon's car in the driveway. I was even more surprised to see him sitting on the couch holding Somaiya.

"Hey, where's Trell?" I asked.

"I don't know, he said he needed to step out for a minute and asked me to watch baby girl."

"Did he say where he was going?"

"No, but it's cool. I needed some time with my niece."

"I know you don't mind, but he should be here."

"Don't sweat it Tae," he said as he stood up to give me a kiss on the forehead.

I sat in the recliner and watched my uncle and daughter making faces at each other.

"Why didn't you ever have kids, Uncle Leon?" I asked.

"Well, there was a time in my life that I wanted them, but I never stayed in one place long enough to have them." He replied.

I laughed, "Oh so basically, you were a player."

"I still am niece, you better ask around," he joked. "In all seriousness, a wife and kids would've been a weakness for me."

"How is that?"

"When I was running the streets, if I had beef they would've come for my family first. I stayed out of most things, but in that life anything can happen."

Any time he brought up his days in the streets, it made me think of my father. I wished that he would've gotten out of the life sooner so that he could be here right now. All of our lives would be so different right now.

"Did anyone ever come after me and mom to get back at daddy?"

"Nah, they just waited to catch Mike slipping."

"It was that simple, huh?"

He silently nodded his head, and I decided to end the conversation there. Part of me felt bad for always asking about my father. I knew very little about his death, and Uncle Leon was the only one I could ask about it. Whatever went down, weighed heavily on my uncle. He silently dismissed himself and took Somaiya to her room. Before I could go back to console him, my phone rang.

"Hello?" I answered.

The automated voice from the county jail began speaking. I assuming it was Ky, I accepted the charges before it could get any farther.

"Tae, baby I need you to come get me." Trell said.

I was so shocked that it took me a second to get my thoughts together.

"What the hell are you doing in the county jail?" I asked angrily.

"I'm not in the jail, I'm in processing next door to the jail. I need you to come get me."

"What the fuck Trell!" I yelled.

By the way he slurred the end of his sentence, let me know that he was drunk.

I sighed, "How could you possibly end up in jail when you're supposed to be home with your daughter?"

"I went to get a drink, and some shit popped off. I'll explain when you get here." He said quickly before hanging up.

I threw my phone across the room in anger, causing Uncle Leon to dart back into the living room.

"Are you okay?" he asked.

"No, Trell got arrested." I replied.

The statement sounded weird. I never thought that I would ever have to say those words to anyone. It was disappointing because he'd done serious time before, and he'd always been adamant about not going back to prison.

"Do you need me to go get him?" Uncle Leon asked.

Normally I wouldn't involve him in something like this, but there was no way I was leaving my house to go pick up that fool.

"Can you please?" I answered.

Uncle Leon kissed me on the forehead, and left to pick up my fiancé. I sat on the couch thinking about what he could've possibly done to get arrested. I was anxious as hell the whole time I waited for them to come home. I knew Trell was downtown so it wouldn't be the quickest trip, but it seemed like time was dragging. In the span of an hour, I managed to clean the kitchen, mop the floors, and fold a load of laundry, and they still hadn't made it back. Then to make matters worse, in the rare moment I wasn't thinking about Trell, I was thinking about Gino. I couldn't shake the image of his body in his car like that, and I hadn't heard from Ky to know how things went with the police.

Right before I started to lose my mind, I heard car doors closing from outside. I had been so anxious for them to come home that I didn't even think about what I was going to do once they came home. However once Trell came inside, I felt myself getting upset.

"Baby, let me at least explain what happened," He pleaded.

"Holla at me when you're sober," I said, "and don't you dare think about coming into our bed that way."

"Tae! I'm sorry." He started to plead his case again, but Uncle Leon stopped him.

"Go upstairs and stay in the guest room tonight," he said. "She just needs0 some time."

Trell followed instructions and wobbled his way up the stairs.

"Why are you being so nice to him?" I asked. "If this were Shaun, you'd be calling Tony and the boys for a cleanup."

"Shaun was a bitch," he replied. "If you didn't lay him down, I would've put two in him my damn self. Trell is different."

"I'm not going to let him disrespect me, Unc."

"Get the respect you deserve, but you have to remember that he lost his brother too."

I had to stop and think. I had been so focused on myself and the baby, that I hadn't stopped to think about how he was dealing with losing Boo. Even after he got upset about it the other day, he just went back to being himself. Upset or not, it still wasn't a reason for him to behave this way. He has a daughter to think about.

I sighed, "I hear you Uncle, but I'm not going to let him get in the habit of pulling this bullshit."

Uncle Leon shook his head, kissed me on the forehead, and went home. I plopped down on the couch and mentally recapped my day. It had been a minute since I'd been this stressed out, and I didn't know how, or where to start, but I was definitely going to have to make some life changes.

## CHAPTER 6

After a few days passed, I found myself wrapped up in my work. I was originally supposed to work from home until I remembered that Trell was off today. Despite trying to suppress my growing frustration with him, I couldn't stop thinking about him being arrested. He was desperately trying to get back on my good side, but it wasn't making a bit of difference. I just didn't want to be around him right now. I was trying to figure out how we went from being happy parents, to being where we are now. All I knew was that we had a lot of work to do if we were going to make it down the aisle, because at this point I wasn't sure that we would.

The thing that bothered me the most, was the fact that I didn't have time to mourn Gino. When my mind wasn't focused on my ridiculous acting fiancé, it was thinking about how G went out. Tonight G's family was having a candlelight service for him. I was pushing back the opening time for everyone so that they could go to the service if they wanted to.

I was deep in my thoughts when I heard a commotion in the club area. Since it was only Envy and I in the building, I ran out of my office to see what was happening. When I got out there Envy was arguing with a tall, model-looking chick, with a long feed in braids that went up into a ponytail. I recognized her from one of the boutiques that Envy and I used to frequent, but she never really spoke. It was a totally different person than the one who was fussing and cussing at Envy. They were talking over one another, so I couldn't really hear what the argument was about, but that woman was pissed.

"Whoa, what's going on?" I asked, standing in between the both of them.

Envy shook her head.

"Just who I was looking for!" The woman shouted, "Your little worker bee over there told me that you weren't here, but I knew that was a lie."

"That's because I knew you were on some bullshit, Aylin!" Envy yelled at her.

I froze as soon as I heard that name, and once I got

a good look at her, I knew exactly who she was. I remembered her from when Trell and I first started dating. When he felt like he wasn't getting enough attention from me, he ran off and kicked it with this chick.

"Aylin, huh?" I asked.

She smirked, knowing that I knew exactly who she was.

"What are you here for?" I questioned.

"You seem irritated sis, you good?" she taunted.

"Nope, just busy." I responded.

"How is La' Trell? Did he make it home okay?"

Hearing her call him by his government name made me sick. While I knew that she was just trying to get me upset, I couldn't stop the anger that was brewing inside of me. How the hell did she know where he was?

"No need to worry about him, boo." I said, "He's in good hands, so you can see yourself out."

I turned on my heels to head back to my office.

"Just tell him that it was good seeing him last night, and your daughter is adorable."

That was enough to stop me in my tracks. If Trell wanted to be an idiot and associate himself with this trash that was on him, but the fact that she felt comfortable enough to mention my daughter was an issue. Clearly she wanted some shit to pop off, and she was about to get all of it. I quickly walked in Aylin's direction. I had all intentions of wiping her smirk off her face, but Kylan came in before I could get to her.

"Is everything okay boss?" he asked.

"I don't know," I replied. "Is it?"

Aylin laughed, "Bye girl, send Trell my love."

She blew a kiss at me, and I lunged at her. Luckily for Aylin, Ky caught me before I could get to her.

"Tae, you don't want to do that," he said. "Women like that don't have shit to lose."

As much as I wanted to wipe the floor with that hoe, he was right. The last thing I needed was to end up with a ridiculous lawsuit, all because I let some bum, get me angry.

"By the way," Ky continued. "I need to speak to you in your office."

I took a deep breath, and went back to my office with Kylan in tow. When we got inside, I sat at my conference table, as he closed the door behind him.

I sighed, "What's up Ky?"

"I found out what happened to Gino."

"Okay," I replied. "What happened?"

"I heard that this nigga Chaos killed Gino," he explained. "Apparently he's a Baltimore nigga that has some ties to King."

"Ugh!" I screamed, "Why won't this man die?"

Every time I think I'm rid of him, he pops up again. I literally put this man in the ground, and he's still causing issues. I started to cry, but I caught myself. When I promised myself that I wouldn't shed any more tears over my bitch ass brother, I meant it.

"Ky, he needs to disappear." I said.

"I'll take care of it." He replied.

I wasn't going to let anyone scare me, or punk me. If they wanted to fuck with me, then let them try it. I'll tell you one thing though; I didn't need anyone doing my dirty work.

"Nah I want to do it myself, I just need you to orchestrate it."

Ky shook his head, "Give me a few days."

"Tonight Ky, I need it done tonight. We have the candlelight service for G, come find me there."

"I don't like this at all, but I got you."

Ky left the office visibly apprehensive about what I asked him to do. I knew I was asking a lot of him, but something told me that this wasn't a random hit. I had no doubt in my mind that King had someone on standby in case he didn't come back. It's no coincidence that some nigga from Baltimore comes in town, and goes after my people. He's probably been scoping out the place for weeks. That was fine, because I was ready for anything that came my way.

I tried to get some work done before going to Gino's service but it was hard to focus. I kept thinking back to the day Trell was shot. After that day, I had a new respect for my security team, especially Gino. If he hadn't did what he did, I'd be a single mother right now, and the fact that he never told meant a lot to me. I wanted to come up with some kind of memorial to put in the club for him. I would have to get with Dani on that, because she was good when it came to creative things like that.

Once I accepted that I wasn't going to get anything done, I got dressed for the candlelight service. I brought a simple black dress and some red pumps to change into. I knew that the service was in a church, but I wasn't sure how dressed up I needed to get. Once I changed, I locked up the club and called a lyft to go the church since it wasn't far.

The scene at Gino's service had to be one of the saddest pictures I'd seen in my life. His mother, Ms. Dorinda was a mess, and from the looks of it, she could barely stand. I hated that she was going through this, and the fact that this is more than likely connected to my issue with King made me feel worse. From what I gathered from G, he and his mother had always been close. He always spoke highly of her, and from the way she was laid out on the front pew of the church, I could tell she thought the world of him as well.

"Hi Ms. D," I greeted, as approached the front of the church.

She sat up to see who was speaking to her, and she smiled.

"Thank you for coming Taela," she said. "It really means a lot to me and the family."

"We're like a family down at the club," I replied. "Gino helped me out when I needed him the most, and he will always have a place in my heart.

I thought back to when Trell was shot, and Gino drove us to the hospital. Some guys would've snitched, quit, or even extorted me after seeing what happened that day, and he never did. After everything was over, he pledged his loyalty to me, and we've never looked back.

"Do you need anything?" I asked her.

She started to cry again.

"All I need is for my baby boy to come through the door."

I hugged her tightly as she started to sob uncontrollably. I couldn't help but to tear up myself. As a mother, I could only pray that I never had to experience the pain she was feeling right now. It almost made me with that I was a little more compassionate towards Rae. Yeah she was erky as hell, but I couldn't imagine how I'd react if Somaiya was taken away from me so suddenly.

Ms. Dorinda pulled away from me when she heard someone come inside the church. She smiled when Kylan walked down the aisle. He quickly hugged and kissed me on the cheek, and went to give Dorinda a long hug.

"I wish I could've been there with him," Ky said.

"Then I'd have two dead sons," she replied, hugging him tighter. "You were there for him when he needed you the most, and that's all that matters."

"I'm going to find out who did this to him, Ma. I

promise you that."

I saw a tear roll down Ky's face, and it did something to me. I'd always seen him as this emotionless military man, and I knew it took a lot out of him to allow people to see him this way. I walked started rubbing his back in an effort to console him, and Ms. Dorinda pulled away from him, so that he could hug me.

"We got him." He whispered in my ear.

He didn't need to go into detail, because I knew exactly what he meant. I just nodded my head and made my rounds to the rest of his family. Before I left, I found the group of people from the club that came out, including Envy and Dani. We gave each other hugs, and took in everything that was going on around us. It really put everything into perspective. Dani and I were in the middle of a ridiculous ass argument, and we were wasting precious time. Life is too short to have petty fallouts with your loved ones. With that thought, my mind instantly went back to Trell. Yes, we had some shit that we had to work through, especially with the surprise guest I got this morning, but we would be okay. We loved each other deeply, and once I figured out what was going on with Aylin, I wanted to get back to us being us.

When I was ready to leave the service, I signaled to Kylan.

"Ya'll leaving already?" Dani asked.

"Yeah, we have somethings to take care of." I stated, "I'll be back around for the club to open tonight."

"Is everything okay?" she asked. "Envy told me about shorty coming through earlier."

"Yeah, everything is fine," I lied. "If Trell calls you, tell him I had to step out for a moment."

"Why would he call me?"

"My phone is on one percent, and my charger is in my car," I lied. "I just don't want him to worry."

She nodded in agreement, and I left with Kylan.

"So what's the deal?" I asked.

"One of my associates found out where he's staying. I can tell him to go in and handle this real quick so that you don't have to."

"No, tell him to go in."

Ky shook his head and started his car. The whole ride over, we sat in silence. I didn't know what was on Ky's mind, but mine was all over the place. I was thinking about Gino dying, I was thinking about Trell being arrested, and I was thinking about my brother being the center of all of this. Most of all I couldn't believe I was about to do this. The thought of it scared me to be honest. Not the thought of killing someone else, but the thought that it was becoming so easy for me. I didn't like it, but if this was what I had to do to get niggas to leave me the fuck alone, then so be it.

When we turned on to the street where the house was, Kylan cut the lights. We parked behind another big black truck.

"Do all of your people ride around in black trucks?" I asked.

"More or less," he replied. "We can't pull shit like this off riding around in a car with big pink bows on it."

I knew he was referring to my white range rover, who I affectionately called kitty. My uncle Leon always told me not to break the law in that car, because I'd be caught immediately.

I smirked and rolled my eyes, "Are you really trying to be funny right now."

He shrugged his shoulders and cut off the car.

"The house is right there," he said, pointing to a house across the street. "My partner is already inside."

"So how do we get in without being seen?"

"My boy Junior left the front door unlocked. You go in first, knock like you're waiting for someone to answer the door, then walk in."

"Okay cool, you gonna stay here?"

"Hell no," he replied. "You think I'mma let you run loose by yourself, Griselda?"

I gave him the "stop playing" face.

"Okay," he continued. "Give it a few minutes, and I'll walk around the back so you can let me in that way."

"Bet."

I reached into my purse and grabbed my gun, and a silencer that I got from Uncle Leon's car. I knew that he would never give me one on his own, so yesterday when he was napping with Somaiya; I went in his car and got one form under his seat. He would notice that it was gone eventually, but I would cross that bridge when I got there.

I got out of the car and walked up to the house. If it was one time I wished I hadn't worn heels, it was now. I felt like every time I took a step, I was bringing more attention to myself. Nonetheless, I walked up to the door, knocked four times, and went inside. The house was pretty nice on the inside, and you could tell it was an Air Bnb by the way it was perfectly decorated. I started looking around, but before I could start exploring too much, I heard Ky tap on the back door. I quickly walked to the back to let him in.

"Where's your boy?" I asked.

"He's down in the basement."

"Cool." I replied, and started walking to the basement door.

Kylan grabbed my arm.

"Chill out, let me go first." He instructed.

I allowed him to walk in front of me and followed him to the basement. All the mental preparing I thought I did in the car went out the window when I saw the man, who I assumed was Chaos, beaten bloody, and tied to a chair. Kylan's homeboy came and dapped him up.

"Tae this is Junior, and Junior this is Tae. She's my boss at the club." Ky explained.

Junior and I shook hands, and I started to feel a little uncomfortable. Here we were exchanging pleasantries, and there was a whole person tied to a chair in front of us.

"So Junior, what's the deal?"

"This lil nigga won't say who sent him, but I know for a fact he's from Baltimore. He works for this punk ass dealer named King."

I walked over to Chaos and got eye level with him.

"Why are you here?" I asked.

He just sat there, breathing heavily.

I chuckled, "Oh you a real one, huh?"

I reached up under my dress and pulled the gun from its holster. I tapped the barrel of the silencer against his temple.

"The man you killed was special to me and my friend over there, but something is telling me that you're not after my friend."

"I ain't got shit to say to ya'll." He spat.

"Oh snap, he's mad ya'll." I joked.

I hit him in his face with the butt of my gun and he screamed. Ky and Junior winced.

"Are you willing to die for this shit?" I asked.

"Fuck you," he said, as he spit out blood.

I shrugged my shoulders and cocked my gun, and took aim.

Kylan came up behind me, "Boss let me handle this clown."

"Nah, this is all me."

"Boss, I don't want you riding in the car with that mess on your outfit."

"Fuck this outfit." I said, before letting off three shots in his chest.

Blood spattered everywhere, and I remembered a time where the mere sight of blood freaked me out. I'd seen so much in the past year that it didn't ever bother me that it I was covered in it.

Ky shook his head and took out his phone, and started typing.

"I'm going to the car," I said, before going up the stairs to leave.

This time, I went through the back door. I didn't want anyone to see me coming out of the house. I damn sure didn't want anyone hearing me so I took off my shoes. When I got in the car, I sat in silence as I came down off the adrenaline high. I hated to admit it, but with all the stress I'd been dealing with, shooting my gun felt like such a release. I finally got a chance to let out my frustration with the craziness that had consumed my life in the past month or so, and it scared me. Mid-thought the car door opened, and spooked the shit out of me, so I pulled my gun. I was relieved to see that it was Ky.

"Whoa, are you okay." He asked, with his hands up.

"Yeah, I'm good," I said. "I'm just a little jittery."

"I had him call your uncle for a clean-up job, but I made sure that he didn't mention us at all."

"That makes me feel better," I said. "At least I know it will be spotless in there."

I took another deep breath.

"I need to get home and sleep." I said.

"I bet, but you know you're gonna have to give me your gun. You got two bodies on it now, and now it has evidence on it since you're running around smacking people with guns."

I sighed, "Here, take it."

Ky reached under his seat and pulled out a plastic bag to place the gun in. He got out of the car to put the gun in Junior's trunk, and then he ran back to his truck.

"He has an incinerator; he'll melt that shit down."

Ky got in the car, and we pulled off. Again, we rode in silence, but I was almost certain that we were thinking about the same thing. The energy in the car was a bit awkward, and I knew it was because of how I handled Chaos. I didn't know if he wanted to talk about it, but I damn sure didn't.

When we got back to the club, I couldn't wait to get in my car and go home. I tried to hurry up and get out of there, but Ky stopped me before I could make a mad dash to my car.

"Burn all that shit you got on," he instructed. "And try not to touch anything. I'll bring you a new gun tomorrow."

"Okay cool," I replied. "One thing before I leave Ky."

"What's that, Tae?"

"If you interfere while I'm handling business again, you're going to find yourself on the wrong end of my piece." I said before slamming the door.

I hated to threaten him but I was serious. In any other situation, I'd just fire his ass but at this point he knew way too much, so if shit went south he would have to be taken care of just like anyone else who crossed me. Hopefully it wouldn't make things weird between us, but I couldn't worry about that at the moment. I needed to get my ass in my truck and go home. Not only did I need shower, but I had some unfinished business with Trell.

## CHAPTER 7

I sat in my car, praying that everyone was sleeping when I went inside. My dress was covered in blood, and even though I had on all black, I was noticeably wet and I knew it would raise some questions. Not to mention, with my luck, Uncle Leon would be posted up in the living room, and there was no way I could get anything past him. The only option I had was to go straight to the bathroom so that I could undress, shower, and bag up my clothes. Once I walked in, I saw my uncle passed out on the couch as expected, so I tip toed past him. I was so busy trying to get to the stairs I didn't think to check the kitchen where Trell was cleaning.

"Why you sneaking through here like that?" he asked, startling me.

"I was trying not to wake Uncle Leon," I said

without turning around.

"What's wrong Tae?" he asked.

I could feel him walking over to me, so I sucked my teeth and went up the stairs. I wished that I was pretending to be mad with him, but that was far from the case. I would be addressing the fact that his bitch rolled up on me in my club, but I needed to shower first. I went into the bathroom, and locked the door. I undressed, and put my clothes in a large rite aid bag I had hidden under my sink. These were the moments I was glad that black people saved all their plastic bags. Not that I kept them around in the event that I needed to get rid of bloody clothes, but it definitely came in handy tonight.

After taking the longest shower in my life, I left the bathroom to find Trell sitting on the bed. He clearly wanted to talk, but I wasn't trying to get into all of that with him. I went straight from the bathroom, to the closet to get my nightclothes.

"So you don't see me sitting right here?" he shouted from the bed.

When he didn't get a response, I heard him walking towards the closet.

"Tae, what the hell is wrong with you?" he asked,

frustrated.

I sighed, "Trell leave me alone. We can talk but not right now."

I tried to leave the closet, but he blocked the doorway.

"Can you move?"

"Are you cheating on me?"

I gave him my 'negro please' look. I didn't know what he was on, but I wasn't in the mood for it tonight. Honestly, the idea was so funny it almost made me laugh.

"What the hell are you talking about?"

"First you come home mad late, and then you go straight to the shower?" he questioned. "I know you're mad at me but damn, Tae!"

"You sound stupid," I replied. "Now move out of my way."

"Tae, talk to me!"

"Aylin came by the club today."

Trell shook his head and took a step back.

"Man, get out my face with that," he said as he left the closet.

I followed him into our bedroom.

"You wanted to talk, right? Let's talk!" I shouted.

"Why did that bitch feel like it was okay for her to come to my club?"

"I don't know, ask her."

"I'm asking you, La' Trell!"

"Stop yelling, you're going to wake up Lil Mama."

I was so irritated by that statement that I punched him in his chest. How dare he use my daughter to try to get out of some bullshit he caused?

"Damn, Tae." He said, grabbing his chest. "I saw her at the bar, but nothing happened."

"How the fuck do you know?" I yelled, "You were wasted!"

Just then, I heard Somaiya crying over the baby monitor. Trell started to go to her room to get her, but I stopped him.

"Don't touch my daughter." I said, before going to get her out of her crib.

I sat in the rocking chair, and rocked my baby girl until she went back to sleep. All I could do was pray that no man ever hurt her the way that men in my life continued to hurt me. That included her father. We needed to finish our conversation, but tonight wasn't the night. Tensions were high between the two of us, and I was still reeling from what happened with Chaos.

After Somaiya went back to sleep, I crawled in the twin bed next to her crib. Trell could have the room tonight, but I needed to be close to my baby.

I opened my eyes, and was surprised to see that it was morning. I was even more surprised to see Trell with Somaiya, rocking her back and forth in the rocking chair. As mad as I was with him, I couldn't help but to smile watching him with her. He was so gentle and calm when he was holding her and every once in a while I'd catch him singing to her. He was a great father; it was him as a partner that needed some work.

"You always seem to beat me to her." I said as I sat up on the bed.

"I know you like to sleep in sometimes, I like to give you some extra time." He replied.

"Thank you, I had a rough night."

"Yeah, I did too. I don't like sleeping alone." He said, "You know we can't keep arguing like this."

"I agree, but don't act like I don't have reason to be upset." I shot back.

He put baby girl back in her crib, and sat on the edge of the bed.

"Look, I went to the bar with some of the guys and

Aylin was there. She tried to push up, and I told her to take her ass on."

"That sounds like some bull shit Trell. Why would she feel comfortable enough to come to my club?"

"She just wanted to cause friction, and clearly it worked."

He was right. I let some chick come in and disrupt my home without giving him the chance to explain himself. She almost broke up something that took us so much time and effort to build, but it wasn't going down like that. I leaned over to give Trell a kiss, but he leaned back.

"Nah, you need to tell me what had you coming home so late last night."

"The memorial for G was last night. I needed to clear my mind afterwards so I went to the cascade at Thomas Polk."

"Next time you need to call. I was worried about you."

I hugged him and kissed him on his cheek. A tiny part of me felt guilty, but I was mostly just happy he bought it. I couldn't tell him where I really was because I didn't want to bring that dark cloud back to our relationship. Trell didn't want to see me in that light and this time it would be different. When I killed Shaun, it was a life or death situation. In my opinion, this was too, but I wasn't too sure that Trell would see it that way. The one mistake I made with Shaun, was telling too many people. The only people who needed to know what happened tonight were the people who were there and god.

I laid my head on Trell's shoulder as he slid his arm around my waist. He looked as if he was thinking hard about something.

"What are you concentrating on over there?" I asked.

He didn't say anything.

"Hello," I said louder, while waving my hand in front of his face.

"Sorry," he said. "I was just thinking that we should get married."

I laughed and flashed my ring, "Did you forget about this?"

"No babe, I mean this weekend." He said, "There's a chapel like two hours away, we can elope."

I knew that he was happy we made up, but there was no way in hell I was going to do some spur of the moment wedding. I would never rob my mother of the chance to watch her only child walk down the aisle.

"Why would we do that without our family there?" I asked. "We need to just set a date."

Trell took a long pause.

"Let's do it on New Year's Eve."

I smiled, "Aww, that was the day we met."

"Nah, that was the day you stopped being mean to me," he laughed.

"Either way, that's only about four months away. Are you sure?"

"I'm positive."

I kissed my fiancé passionately and straddled him. I started to take of his shirt but he stopped me.

"We still got two weeks left until you're in the clear." Trell said.

"I don't give a damn." I replied.

I proceeded to take off his shirt, and kissed him on his neck and chest. He helped me out of my top, and began caressing my breasts. We were both moving quickly because we knew we were on borrowed time. I helped him out of his pants, and began tasting him. He grabbed my braids with one hand, and gently guided my head as it bobbed up and down. Once I was ready for him, I stood up so that I could take off my shorts.

"Do you want me to get on top?" he asked.

"Nah, I got this," I replied.

I slowly lowered myself onto him. I moved my hips a little, just to make sure there wasn't any pain. Even though I didn't have a vaginal birth, I was still nervous about hurting myself. However once I realized that it didn't hurt, I started riding him faster. It seemed like it had been so long since we'd made love and it felt amazing. I tried my best not to moan loud, so I didn't wake up the baby but it wasn't working. I started to pick up my pace, and Trell grabbed on to my hips as I moved them in circular motion. In no time, I could feel myself starting to come.

"Oh shit babe," I moaned.

Trell put his hand over my mouth.

"You better not wake her up before I finish," he said.

I started bouncing up and down, and I knew that his ass was about ready to tap out. I was just praying that we didn't fall out of this little ass bed before he did. After a minute or two, he started to grip my thighs tightly as he came. Feeling satisfied, I laid on the next to him as he wrapped his arms around me. Like clockwork, Trell started falling asleep. I knew it was only a matter of time before he started snoring in my ear, so I closed my eyes so I could beat him to sleep. All I could think as I drifted off to sleep was "I hope my ass didn't get pregnant again."

I almost forgot Somaiya was in the room until she started crying. I looked at the clock on the wall, and realized we'd been sleep for damn near an hour. I slid out of the bed, got dressed, and picked up Somaiya out of her crib. He diaper was wet, so o took her to the changing table so I could change her. I started singing 'You Are my Sunshine' to her, because it took her mind off getting her diaper changed, which she hated. I tried to be as quiet as possible so we didn't wake Trell, but he was such a light sleeper, it didn't matter. He sat up and smiled as he watched me rocking and singing to our baby girl.

"I'm going to miss seeing this while I'm in Atlanta." Trell said.

"We're going to miss you too," I replied. "You'll only be gone two days though, so it wont be too bad. Why are you going down there?"

"I want to start spending more time in my ATL store. That's the only store that doesn't have family managing it."

"True, but I think we should take a trip with our family. You know I love it there, especially the nightlife."

"You ever thought about opening something up there?"

"Not really," I replied. "We're doing well here, but I don't feel like we're established enough for all of that."

"It could be a future move, but if you're going to do it, now would be the time to start mapping it out."

He was right. I was so focused on the present, that I had no idea of what I wanted to do next. Tae's Place Charlotte was on its way up, and maybe Tae's Place Atlanta was my next move.

"I think you're right. I can start training Angie to run it for me."

"Angie?" He responded. "What about Envy?"

"Well I'd like a family member to run it, kind of like you have your stores set up."

"She's been your family for ten minutes, Tae."

"She's still family though." I said. "Why are you endorsing Envy so hard?

"I think she would be a good fit," he replied. "She held shit down while you were gone. Not to mention,

Envy is from Atlanta, and she comes from the club scene down there."

"No, she comes from the strip club scene down there."

"It's the same damn thing," he argued. "You should do what you want, but I think it would be a huge mistake not to have Envy manage the club."

"Look I get that everyone is leery of Angie, but that's my sister. If no one is going to have my back, she will."

"Hey, it's your club," He said before kissing me on my forehead. "I gotta get ready to make this drive."

"Okay, I love you."

I took Somaiya, who was now sleeping, and went downstairs to my home office. I put her in her crib, and logged into my computer. I only would have a little bit of time to get somethings ready before I went in to work later on.

Walking into the club that evening, I felt great. Trell and I were finally feeling like we were back to normal, and I worked all day on a business proposal for Dani. After Trell and I spoke about his store in Atlanta, I gave some more thought into opening a second location. With the Charlotte club still being new, I knew it would be some time before I would be able to make it happen, but I could start working on it. I also wanted to get Dani's opinion on it. Even though she would be gone by the time I opened it up, I still respected her opinion.

When I came in, Dani was sitting in one of the VIP sections, talking to Envy. It looked like they were having a meeting about something, so I quietly took a seat next to envy. I didn't think about it before, but it would be good for Envy to hear what I had planned too, since she would be here far longer than Dani would.

"Hey T, I was just helping Envy with some of the details for the charity event." Dani greeted.

"That's good to hear," I replied, with a tad bit of sarcasm.

After the opposition I caught from her in the beginning of the planning process, I couldn't help but to catch a slight attitude. Why argue with me if you were just going to step in anyways? I didn't have time to relive that argument, so I just let it go.

"Can I interrupt for a second?" I asked. "I want to show you two something I've been working on."

I pulled out the proposal from my workbag and

handed it to Dani. She began thumbing through it slowly.

"What is this exactly?" She asked.

"Well, I was thinking of opening up a small spot in Atlanta."

Envy got excited, "Oh shit, in my hometown?"

"Yes ma'am. It'll be a while before I can start making any moves out there, but we need to start preparing now if this is going to work."

Dani continued looking through the proposal, while Envy peered over her shoulder. The silence as they both reviewed each page made me uneasy. I didn't know how I thought they would react, but I wasn't expecting the silence. Dani shut the proposal and sighed. I waited eagerly for her to give her opinion.

"The only thing I'm trying to figure out is how you plan to do all this from another state."

"Well I would be down there for the first couple weeks, but I was going to ask Angie to run it."

Dani gave a sarcastic laugh, and Envy sat back in her seat.

"Why not have Envy run it?" Dani asked.

"Well she doesn't really have the experience in management."

"Excuse me?" Envy chimed in.

"I got it, E." Dani said, before directing her energy back to me. "Envy has been helping me run shit since you've been gone."

"Exactly, she's been helping you. Not running it on her own."

"You don't have the new one opening for another two years. By the time that comes around she'll be running this place."

"I want to keep it in the family, and Angie is family."

Dani laughed, "You're joking right."

"Why would I be?"

"You just met her!" she said.

"So what, that doesn't make her any less of my sister!" I yelled.

"You're being ridiculous, and extremely naive, Tae. I'd say I was surprised, but this wouldn't be the first time."

"Why do you even care Dani? You're on your way out."

At this point, I was over Dani fighting me at every turn. I needed her to support me on this, so that we can make this work.

"Can we stop talking about me like I'm not here?" Envy asked. "I feel like this is a total slap in the face. I deserve to run the new club."

"Envy you're going to be the manager once Dani leaves, why isn't that enough?"

"Would that be enough for you Tae?" she shot back.

"If you don't like it, you can always leave."

Envy chuckled, "Fuck this, I make more money dancing anyways."

Envy grabbed her belongings and left.

"If she goes, I'm going with her." She said.

I knew she was pulling my card, but she knew that I would fold. The bottom line was that I needed Dani right now. I knew I would be in and out because of Somaiya, and I needed the back up.

I sighed, "You can hire her back if you want, but she's your responsibility."

Dani rolled her eyes and ran after Envy. This was so ridiculous to me. I hated that an attempt to bring my sister in on my dream, meant that I was turning my back on my friends. It wasn't meant as a slight to anyone, but at the end of the day, this was my shit and I could do what I wanted. If they didn't like it, then that was on them. I knew that Envy wouldn't understand, but I was surprised at Dani. It was another instance of her showing her ass, and I was starting to get sick of it. As apprehensive as I was about it before, I was now more than ready for her to leave so that I could be done with her and Envy for good.

## CHAPTER 8

Since I only had four months to plan my wedding, and I had recently cut off my best friend I called my mom for backup. I didn't know how receptive she would be to coming back down since it had only been a couple of weeks since she'd left. Then when I considered how irritated she was with me when she did, I was skeptical that she'd actually agree. Luckily, she was super excited and caught the first plane out of BWI. I hadn't told to her about my falling out with Dani and Envy, and that was mainly because I wasn't prepared to hear her lectures. I was already getting it bad enough from Trell. Of course, his stupid ass agreed with Envy and Dani. He didn't say I was being naïve, but from our conversation, it was implied. He felt like it was too early to let Angie in on anything business related. I couldn't figure out why everyone had beef with me cutting my sister in on the business. Yes, it was a new relationship and we were still learning each other, but she was still my sister at the end of the day.

Pettiness aside, I was a little disappointed in the fact that my girls wouldn't be here to help me with the wedding planning. I had always envisioned the three of us doing this together, but the show must go on. My mother and I would be sharing this moment, and that was perfect.

Once she was settled and rested after her flight, we headed over to a little bakery downtown. I didn't think much of it at first, but I quickly regretted not choosing a more hands on activity for us to do. My mother had the tendency to pry into my personal life, and a cake tasting provided just enough down time for her to do just that.

"Is Dani going to meet us there?" she asked.

"No, she's not coming." I replied, hoping to end the conversation.

"Why not?"

I sighed, "We're not speaking."

"I know, I was just waiting on you to tell me."

"How did you know?" I asked.

"How do you think I know?" she answered.

I rolled my eyes. I should've known that Dani would call her mother and tell her everything. Our mothers are gossip buddies, so I'm sure Ms. Sonia called my mom as soon as she hung up with Dani.

"Ma they're on one, and I don't need that kind of negativity right now." I explained.

"I just don't understand why she couldn't come with us because of an argument. You two are like sisters."

"We're like sisters, but that doesn't make us sisters."

My mother chuckled. She always did that when she got irritated.

"You know what; the truth of the matter is that you were wrong. I know it's your business and you're going to do what you want, but Envy deserves to take over the new club."

"I'll tell you like I told them, Angie is family."

"Barely!" she said, raising her voice. "You just met her, and I'm sorry Taela but I don't trust her."

"I'm not talking about this anymore."

"You're always running Tae, and it's gonna get old eventually. You ran from Rae back home, and now you're running from whatever guilt you're harboring about your brother being missing."

I wanted to deny that my mother was right, but I couldn't. Sure, I was excited to have Angie in my life, but maybe I was doing a little too much. The fact of the matter was that I didn't know her that well and it may be a good idea to keep her out of my business matters until I can fully vet her.

"You're right. I'm still not happy about how Dani came at me, but I probably should slow down with Angie."

"That's all I was trying to say," she said. "Get this shit right Taela, I hope to see Dani and Envy when we go look for your dress."

Before I could get another word out, the woman from the bakery came in the room to check on us. I asked her to pack up some samples for Trell, so he could try them when he got home. After the tasting, I needed to run to the club. I was glad that I got my mother a rental car so I didn't have to go home first. I was having a staff meeting this afternoon, and I wanted to talk to Envy and Dani before it started. It was time we all got on the same page, and quit letting petty shit get between us. While Envy and I had only been friends for a little while, I'd known Dani my whole life, and I hated that the place we were in. I think we needed to sit down and hash out our differences no matter how long it took.

When I got to the club, most of the staff was awaiting for me in the VIP areas. I went back to my office and set my belongings down at my desk, and peeked my head into Dani's office. She was digging through her personnel files obviously looking for something.

"Is everything okay, D?"

She looked up at me and rolled her eyes. As much as it irritated me, I didn't feed in to it. That's how most of our arguments escalated.

"What's wrong Danita?" I asked.

"I'm looking for Terrell's information. She went to the store for me an hour ago, and she hasn't come back yet."

Terrell was one of the bottle servers, and I couldn't see her leaving work unless there was something going on with her daughter. Under normal circumstances I would be a little nervous, but I could feel myself panicking. With all the mess going on around here lately, the slightest thing raised a red flag. I had taken care of the goon King sent, so I knew this couldn't be him, but I was still worried that something could've happened to her.

"If you get in contact with her let me know." I instructed, "I'm going to run the meeting and we can pull up on her at home if we need to."

"Sure, Taela." She replied.

I could tell that she still wasn't here for me, but we could take care of that later. Right now, I had a meeting to run, and we needed to figure out what was going on with Terrell. I went to the main area to address my employees.

"Good afternoon everyone, is everyone here?" I asked.

"I sent Mia to take the trash out," Envy said. "I'll go get her."

As Envy left to grab our missing bottle girl, I started the meeting.

"I just want to start by thanking every one for holding things down while I was out on maternity leave–"

"Tae!" Envy screamed.

I sprinted to the back of the club and out the door. Mia and Envy were hugging each other and crying.

"What happened?"

Mia pointed at the dumpster. I peeked over and saw Terrell's body inside. I could tell that she'd been stabbed, but I also could tell that she wasn't gone yet. I quickly took out my phone and called an ambulance. By the time I got off the phone with them, Dani had come outside.

"What the hell is going on Tae?" she asked.

"I don't know, D." I said tearing up. "This shit is crazy."

I went inside to address the rest of the staff who was still sitting in the VIP area waiting for me to come back.

"Listen up everyone," I said. "We're going to postpone this meeting. You're all free to go."

A few of them tried to ask me questions, but I dismissed them and went in my office. I couldn't believe that this was happening. I prayed that she made it through because I didn't know what I would do if another person who worked here came up dead. The issues I was trying so hard to avoid, seemed to be coming my way whether I laid low or not. I felt like an ass for thinking that way, but it was the truth. In the middle of trying to figure out what to tell my staff, I heard a knock on the door.

"The ambulance is here, Taela." Dani said.

I took a deep breath and followed her out the back door. Watching them put Terrell in the back of that truck did something to me. The thought of what could possibly happen, took me back to when I lost my father. Her daughter was around the same age I was when he passed, and I would hate for her to have to grow up feeling like I did. After getting her in the truck, the paramedic let us know that they would be taking her to Novant Presbyterian.

"I'll drive us over if you want," Dani offered.

"Okay," I replied, still in a daze.

The ride to the hospital was awkward as hell. I wanted to spill my feelings to Dani right then and there, but I felt like it wasn't the right time. Instead, I thought about how I was going to explain to my staff what happened. Once they found out that another one of their coworkers died while working for us, they would jump ship. Hell, I wouldn't blame them if they did. I wouldn't work somewhere knowing that employees were dropping left and right.

"None of this is your fault." Dani said as if she was reading my mind.

I wish I could agree with her, but if she knew what happened with Gino, she'd be singing a different tune.

I replied, "That makes me feel better, but I can't say that I believe it right now."

"I know you feel like this is some kind of karma for the bullshit with your brother, but it isn't. Sometimes these things just happen."

I took a deep breath. What I wanted to do was spill everything that had been happening behind the scenes, but it was too heavy. Me and Ky said we wouldn't speak about it, and I planned to stick to it. Besides, with the way D had been moving, I wasn't one hundred percent sure that I could still trust her with something like that. So, I just bottled it up and tried to take my mind off of it.

When we got inside the hospital, we went to the nurse's desk and explained to them who we were. She pointed us in the direction of two women who she called the family. I assumed they were her sisters, because they looked exactly like her.

"Hi I'm Taela," I said introducing myself. "Terrell works Dani and I at the club."

The eldest of the two women stood to give me and Dani a hug.

"Hi, I'm her mother Tami." She replied.

I was shocked at how young she looked. She was another clear example of how black don't crack.

"Do know who did this?" she asked.

"No ma'am. When I got to the club, she was already on her way to the store. I'm guessing whoever did this, caught her on her way out."

Tami started to sob and I wrapped my arm around he4r.

"Have the doctors come out to talk to you yet?" I asked.

"No they haven't. The nurses said she's in surgery, and they would let us see her when she was out."

"Well, I'll be here with ya'll until then." I replied.

We all sat in the waiting room restlessly. The longer we sat there waiting, the more anxious I got. I figured that she had lost a lot of blood judging by how much was in the dumpster, but I didn't think that the surgery would take as long as it was taking. After waiting about three hours, a doctor came out. He went to the nurse's station, and a nurse pointed him in our direction. Tami immediately stood up when she spotted him.

"Ms. Brown?" the doctor asked.

"Yes, I'm Mrs. Brown," she replied. "Can I see my daughter now?"

He sighed, "I'm sorry to inform you that your daughter didn't make it."

Tami and Ari began hugging each other while crying hysterically, and Dani and I just stared at each other. I couldn't believe that death had plagued our club family once again.

"Would you like to say your goodbyes?" he said.

Tami shook her head yes, but Ari refused to go.

"I can't see my sister that way," Ari said.

"Tami if you don't want to go alone, I'll go with you." I offered.

"It's okay, I want to be alone with my baby." Tami replied.

I hugged her tightly.

"I will cover any funeral costs you have. Just call me when it's time to make the arrangements."

"I probably won't have one," she replied. "We don't have any family; my girls are all I have."

"Well I'll bring you all some money for her daughter."

"Thank you," she said.

Tami hugged me tightly again, and followed the

doctor back to view her daughter's body. Dani and I hugged Ari one last time before leaving. The car ride home was a silent one. I was trying to figure out what I was going to tell my staff. I also needed to call Ky to see what he could find out. My trigger finger was itching and whoever did this, was going to pay.

## CHAPTER 9

Once news of Terrell's passing hit, it changed the mood of the club. Business was running as usual, but the overall morale was at an all-time low. I still needed to hire another bottle girl, but I didn't have the energy to begin the process. Until that was done, Dani and I would have to help where were needed. I didn't know how long it would be before I got a replacement for her, because I'd been all over the place since everything went down. I'd been racking my brain trying to figure out what happened, and Kylan hadn't heard anything yet about who did it. It made me wish that I had camera's installed in the back of the club. All of this would be over with, and I would know who the hell is lurking around my dumpsters.

After a few days, I decided to clear my mind and do some dress shopping. It took some convincing, but I was able to get Dani and Envy to come with me. Well, I convinced Envy, and she agreed to make Dani come with her. She still wasn't here for me in any way at all. She'd even resorted to calling my mother to check on the baby. I figured it would be a good time for us all to get somethings off our chest and make up. The only issue was that I also invited Angie. I told her to come an hour after I told Envy to get there, because I knew that whatever conversation we had, needed to be done before she got there.

When my girls arrived, I was having mixed emotions. Envy was her typical bubbly self, but Dani came in looking like she would rather be anywhere else.

"Hey ladies!" I greeted.

"Hey boo," Envy replied while giving me a hug and kiss.

"Hello Taela." Dani said dryly.

"I asked ya'll to come here for two reasons. The first one being that I need to apologize. I've been on a rampage lately, and I hate that I've hurt you both the way that I have."

"Do you honestly understand why we're upset?" Dani asked. "We held down the fort while you were gone, and you came back and acted like it was nothing. Then you start letting your sister in on the business and you just met her."

"I admit that it was messed up," I replied. "I was over excited, and I see that now. I'm going to keep her out of the business."

"What about the club in Atlanta?" Envy asked.

"That's a long way off, but when we're ready to start working on it for real, we can discuss you running it."

As much as I just wanted to make Envy's week by telling her she would definitely be managing the club, I couldn't. She wasn't ready, and I trusted her to run the club with me there, but not all the wat in Atlanta. Since it would be some time before I had to figure that out, I would definitely be watching her to see if she'll be ready.

"I can respect it; I just didn't like how it was brought to us," Envy replied.

"I know I've been on one lately, and I think I came back to work too fast. My mom thinks I'm dealing with postpartum depression, but I think I'm just a little overwhelmed."

"Look, whatever you have going on, know that were

here for you," Dani said. "You have at least admit that you were wildin' for showing her the books."

"Damn, I said I was tripping." I said. "But now that we've gotten that out of the way I need ya'll to help me find this wedding dress."

"Wait a minute," Dani said as she looked around. "I was so bent on getting my apology that I forgot where we were. Did ya'll set a date?"

"Right, I didn't know ya'll set a date." Envy chimed in.

"We just did a few weeks ago. It's going to be New Year's Eve."

"So let's get to it!" Envy replied. "You know I love dressing you."

"We can't start until Angie gets here.

Dani and Envy rolled their eyes at the mention of my sister. I wished it wasn't so much animosity with them. I didn't anything popping off while I'm planning my wedding.

"Does she really need to be here?" Dani asked.

"Don't start, D. That's my sister."

"As long as she doesn't start with me, we're good."

I hugged my friends and hoped that things were on the way to getting things back to normal. When we pulled away from our embrace, I noticed that Dani had tears in her eyes.

"You okay?" Envy asked.

"Ya'll don't know how much I've needed this, especially after Terrell. That shit hasn't been sitting right on my heart."

"I know," Envy replied. "That whole thing was a little too close to home for me. With Gino he got caught slipping at home, Tee was just trying to go to the store."

"When they find the person who did this to her it's gonna be crazy."

"Can we not talk about this right now?" I asked.

Not only were they killing my mood, but I also had Ky on the job already. I was just hoping that he would find Terrell's killer before the police did.

Right when the tension of speaking about Terrell started to die down, Angie walked in and kicked it back up.

"Hey ya'll." She said, visibly confused.

I didn't mention to her that I was inviting my girls, because I didn't have to. This was my moment, and if they all cared about me like they say they do, they could manage to play nice for an hour or two.

"Hey sis, we were just about to start looking at dresses."

"Cool, is everyone here going to be in the wedding?" She asked.

I sighed, "Yes. Dani and Envy are going to be in the wedding."

"So you're cool with them again."

Dani laughed, "I know you're new here, but we aren't going anywhere fam."

"Are you sure about that?" Angie responded. "Not even a week ago, you were out of here."

"I'm here now, and if it bothers you that much you can leave the same way you came in."

Envy laughed hysterically, and I rolled my eyes. This is exactly what I didn't want to happen. I knew that if one of them started, then it was going to go left immediately. I wasn't expecting Angie to be the one to kick some bullshit off.

"Get your girl Tae," Angie said.

"Ang, you came in starting shit. You know damn well they wouldn't be here if we weren't good."

Angie rolled her eyes and sighed, "Fine, it's your wedding."

There was no way I was going to let them ruin this

day for me. The last thing I wanted was for my wedding memories to be overshadowed by arguing. I sighed and made my way to the showroom to start looking at the dresses. I knew that I wanted a mermaid style dress, but other than that, I was clueless. Envy was able to find a couple that I liked, so I tried those on. They were cute but they didn't really move me. My mother always said that when you find your wedding dress, you'd know because it'll move you to tears. None of them had that effect on me so I decided to give it a rest for the day. It was a great distraction from everything going on, but I needed another outing to decide.

"I think we need to wrap this up, ya'll." I said.

"Aww I'm sorry you didn't find anything you liked. I tried to help you out girl," Envy replied.

"It's cool, we just have to come back out. I think I'll bring my mother with us next time. She usually is pretty helpful."

"Well just let us know, and we'll be here." Envy said.

"See you later?" Dani asked.

"Yeah I'll be in." I replied.

I hugged both Envy and Dani before they hurried

out the door, leaving Angie and I to talk. I could tell that she was upset about my girls being here, but I really didn't understand why. She had to know that we would be making up at some point, especially with us working together. My relationship with them would always be different from our relationship. I just needed her to be my sister and that was it.

"Are you okay Ang?" I asked.

Angie sucked her teeth.

"What's the problem?"

"I just don't understand how you could just make up with them so fast," She said with frustration. "They disrespected you."

"I can't say that I was innocent at all. We all did some shit, apologized, and moved on."

"So what's gonna happen when I start working at the club? Am I supposed to just deal with Dani and her attitude?"

"Well, we need to talk about that." I replied. "I think I'm gonna train Envy to run the Atlanta club."

"Oh wow," Angie said before storming out of the dress shop.

I followed her out the door.

"Angie, let me explain!" I called.

"What do you need to explain Tae?" She asked. "You've shown me where your loyalty lies."

"What the hell are you talking about?"

"Now that you got your friends back, you're gonna push me to the damn side? I see you Tae, and you don't have to worry about me."

"Angie, this right here is what I was trying to avoid. You are my sister, my blood! I can't lose you like I almost did them."

"You know what it's cool. You wanna keep your business and personal separate, and I get it."

"Yes, that's it. It has nothing to do with my friends. I just think that we should focus on our relationship as sisters for now."

Angie took a deep breath. As much as she wanted to get into the club business, I knew that she knew that I was right. We were still building our relationship, and that was more important than going into business together.

"I understand. We'll just work on our sisterly relationship, and I'll try to do better with getting along with Dani."

I gave my sister a hug. I was happy that we were able to get past this. I could tell that she was still upset about not being included in the Atlanta club, but she would get over it eventually. Right now, I just needed everyone to focus on this wedding. We only had a little bit of time to get it together, and I wanted everything to be perfect.

# CHAPTER 10

Since clearing the air with my girls, the vibe at the club was a lot better, and the staff noticed it too. The change in morale was definitely back to normal after losing two of our own. It took a lot of damage control to keep our staff from quitting, especially the bottle girls. While most people viewed Gino's death an unfortunate incident, Terrell's hit a little different. She was murdered right behind the club, so a lot of them were a bit shaken up after that. However, in true boss fashion, Dani and I were able to get them to hang in there with us, and I'm sure the fact that we were back on speaking terms sold it for them.

The only person missing from the place was Ky. He'd been in full investigation mode since everything went down with Terrell. We needed to figure out why this happened before the police found out who killed her. I wanted to take them out myself. So when I got a phone call and saw Ky's name pop up I couldn't answer it fast enough.

"What's good Ky?" I said.

"I found out that info for you." He responded.

"So, what's the word?"

"Chaos had a partner down here named Will. He figured out that you had something to do with him being murdered so he caught Tee outside of the club on some get back shit."

"Where is he? I'm ready."

"My homie has space he uses for shit like this, all you gotta do is say the word, and I'll handle it."

"You know me, I don't need no one doing my dirty work. Figure out where he's gonna be, and we'll run down on him."

Ky sighed, "Okay, I'll get Junior to track his movements and get back to you."

"Okay Ky. Junior is your homeboy, so if he fucks this up it's on you."

"Don't worry boss, we got you."

I hung up the phone, and was shocked to see Uncle Leon standing in my office doorway.

"Hey Uncle!" I greeted.

I was trying to act normal but he wasn't buying it. He shut my office door and sat in front of my desk. I could tell by the look on his face, he heard what I was talking about with Kylan.

"I don't know what you're about to do, but you need to stop and think." He said.

"What do you mean?" I replied, while avoiding eye contact.

"Taela McCray, you think I'm stupid."

"I don't think you're stupid. I know you just heard the tail end of a suspect conversation, but it's all good Unc."

"Tae I come from the damn streets, and I know street shit when I hear it. I know you're upset about your friend but this aint it, Baby Girl."

"They're killing my people Uncle Leon, and I'm sick of people thinking they can mess with me."

"You're running a nightclub, not the got damn cartel Tae. There are other ways."

"Nah, this is my way. It's been working for me so far."

"Has it really? Not too long ago you killed your own damn brother!"

I took a deep breath to calm down. I wanted to go

off on him so bad. He knew how much that fucked me up, and he was the last person I ever thought would throw it in my face.

"You know what Uncle Leon, I'm going to do this my way and that's it."

"Learn from your father and brother's mistakes. This shit will catch up with you, and you better hope it doesn't cost you your life." He said before leaving.

I rolled my eyes and went back to balancing my books. I didn't have time for his bullshit. I was handling this no different than he would if I were asking him to, so I didn't understand what the big deal was. Honestly, it didn't matter what he said, I was going to do what I felt was necessary.

With everything going on, my mind was such a mess. I decided to cut out early and get home to my family. I missed them like crazy, and I'd been working so much that I hadn't really had time to spend time with them.

When I got home, it made me happy to see Trell and Somaiya on the couch sleeping together. At four months old, she finally looked like me. I was excited because at first she looked like her father spit her out. She gradually started looking like me over time. I tried to snap a picture of them, but I forgot to turn my flash off and Trell woke up.

"You taking pictures of me and my daughter?" he asked groggily.

I laughed, "Ya'll were so cute I couldn't resist. I'm going to send it to your mom."

He rolled his eyes and stood up to give me a kiss.

"How was work?" he asked.

"It was okay, we're getting back in the swing of things. I still need to hire a new bottle girl though," I replied. "How was your day?"

"I just kicked it here with lil mama. Your uncle was here earlier, but he seemed like he wasn't really in a good mood."

I had to laugh inside because I knew exactly what was wrong with him. Of course, he's walking around outing because for once I'm not hanging on his every word. I wasn't about to get into that with Trell though.

"Did you eat?" I asked, changing the subject.

"Nah I was about dig in to some of the leftovers from last night, but Somaiya started crying."

"I'll make us some plates." I replied.

Trell gave me another kiss on the cheek and went to put Somaiya in her bassinet. I warmed up some of the leftover baked pork chops and gravy, rice, cabbage, and corn on the cob I'd made the night before. I made plates for Trell and I, and poured us both a glass of wine. After he put the baby down, he joined me in the dining room for dinner.

"It's been a minute since we were able to sit and have dinner like this," he said with a smile.

"I know, things have been crazy at the club" I replied.

"Yeah they've been having you on the late night shift a lot lately."

I gave him a side eye. It felt like he was implying something that he just wasn't saying, and if he kept it up it was going to be an argument. I had enough on my mind without him starting his bullshit, so I chose to let it go.

"Well, it's just taking me some time to get re adjusted to everything. Once I'm acclimated, it'll be better."

"I assumed that's what it was. I'll be glad to have you home more."

Trell leaned over to give me a kiss as my phone chimed. It was Ky letting me know that they spotted Will at the club. He was bold as hell for coming in there like he didn't just take out one of my girls. I told Ky not to let him leave the club, and I would be there as soon as possible. I really didn't want to leave Trell, since this was the first time I'd been able to spend time with him all week. However the sooner we could take care of this shit, the better.

"Is everything okay?" Trell asked in the middle of me responding to Ky.

"Yeah I think so, I gotta go back to the club to fix some shit."

"Isn't Dani there? Why can't she fix it?" he asked.

"Envy is running things tonight, and I need to check on her."

"You need to check on your family." Trell said under his breath.

"What was that La' Trell?" I asked, knowing damn well what he said.

"Nothing, go to the club and handle your business," he said. "We can talk about your fucked up priorities later."

Trell picked up his plate and went upstairs to finish eating. I wanted to go after him, but I didn't really have a valid argument. He was right. I had been so consumed with putting out fires at the club that I'd been slacking with my relationship. I always made sure I was there for Somaiya, but I hadn't really been spending a lot of time with Trell. Once I took care of this last bit of business, I would be able to focus more.

After cleaning up my kitchen, I went to the club to meet up with Ky. I made sure to go through the back entrance so that I couldn't be seen. The second if the staff knew I was there, they'd start asking me all types of questions, and I wasn't in the mood for that. I knew that he didn't come here for nothing. Either he was trying to scope out his next victim, or he was gunning for the main target, which was me unfortunately. I didn't matter anyways because we had the drop on him, and he was going to be dealt with.

I chilled in my office until it was closing time, and waited for Kylan to text me. His job was to take Will out of the back entrance and wait for me there. I wanted him to die in the same place Terrell did. Once I heard my phone go off, I grabbed my gun and silencer, and slid out the back door. Will was laid out on the concrete, clearly after getting into it with Ky. I honestly didn't know why anyone tried it with him. He was big as shit, and he made it clear that he was a trained killer. He was the last person I'd would want to piss off if I was a man.

"Well, what do we have here?" I asked sarcastically.

"This is the lil nigga that killed Tee." Ky informed.

I kneeled down so that I was on Will's level. He looked pitiful as shit, and I'm sure he was wishing he never got himself in this mess to begin with. I was hoping I could get some information out of him about why this was happening. I knew that King would have some sort of backup plan, but I thought they would be gunning for me directly. This shit was way too calculated. You would think that someone who was still living was running the show.

"So here's what's going to happen," I instructed. "You're going to tell me who sent you all the way down south to mess with me, and you can go on about your business."

"If Chaos didn't tell you, what makes you think I'mma talk?" He shot back.

"You're going to tell me because you value your life."

Will looked as if he was thinking about it.

"Man, I aint telling you shit. You can't kill me out in the open like this."

I laughed, "Who's gonna check me, boo? I'll have

you cleaned up before the five a.m. trash pickup."

"All I'm gonna tell you is you need to watch the people in your club, and that comes from my boss."

"I don't believe you," I replied. "My team is solid."

"Not as solid as you think. Now do what you're gonna do to me, because I'm not telling you who sent me."

"Look, I'm not gonna argue with you."

I stood up, and aimed my gun down at Will.

"This is your last chance to tell me." I commanded.

"I aint got shit to say." He retorted.

I pulled the trigger, and watched his body jump as I put two in his chest. I didn't know if there were more people on the way, but I knew that I was finished with this. I needed to get back to the shit that mattered, and that was my family. I handed my gun to Ky, and went back inside to my office.

"Get someone you trust to clean this up. I'm not coming in for a few days, so don't call me unless it an emergency." I said before going inside.

I took a deep breath as I mentally processed all of this. I needed to watch myself, because this was a risky ass move, even with a silencer. It's one thing to kill someone indoors, but doing that shit outside my club shook me up a little. I guess it's a good thing I didn't get those cameras installed after all.

## CHAPTER 11

Trying to move on the next day as if nothing happened the night before was so hard. I was starting to become physically drained with everything going on. Not for nothing, I was getting hit from all fronts. I was hoping the situation with the club was finished now that Chaos and Will were out of the way. My big thing now, was to get my family in a better place. He wasn't really speaking to me, and it was Boo's birthday, so he was in a terrible mood. I tried to get him to take a day off and chill with me, but he insisted on going to work. Afterwards he was going to meet up with some old friends to celebrate Boo. It was kind of eating at me too, since he died because he wouldn't kill me like King wanted. I just hated that it was hurting Trell so bad.

With that in mind, I needed to make sure that

things at the house were running smoothly so Trell didn't have anything to worry about. My plan for the day was to clean up, and spend time with Angie. I hadn't seen her since we went dress shopping, so she was going to come over and chill with Somaiya and me. It didn't seem like she was still upset about the Atlanta club, but I couldn't say that I knew her well enough to know when she was hiding something from me. I just hoped that it wouldn't cause a rift between us so soon in our relationship.

I told Angie that I would make lunch for us, so I changed and fed Somaiya, and got in the kitchen. I wanted something a little more filling than a sandwich, so I made some quick chicken fajitas with some Spanish style rice. I also made some margaritas for us, while making sure to leave some for my mother. She was still in town, and I knew she would have an attitude if she came downstairs and saw that I didn't at least save her a margarita.

I was able to get short break before Angie knocked on the door. I was nervous at first but when she greeted me with her usual hug and kiss, I loosened up.

"What's up sister?" she greeted cheerfully.

"Nothing much, I'm just trying to keep shit

together," I replied. "If it's not something at the club, it's something with my relationship."

"Ya'll arguing again?"

"I wish we were arguing," I said. "He's giving me the silent treatment right now."

"Damn, the way he got you on a pedestal I would've never seen that coming."

"I don't know about all that, but he feels like my priorities are fucked up. This has kind of been an issue since we've been together."

"So what are you going to do to show him different? Something is going to have to change if you want him to speak to you again."

"I'm off for the next couple of days so I'm sure we'll spend time together while I'm home."

"Nah girl, why don't you do something special for him tonight? Put lil mama down a little early, and spend some time with him."

"I'll see what I can make happen." I said to end the conversation. "What's going on with you?"

"Ehh, not much. I'm trying to be permanently transferred down here for work, but my boss is tripping. I may have to go back home soon."

"Damn, you can't extend your leave anymore?"

"I put the request in, but now I have to see if the Hornets have room for me down here." She replied. "Speaking of the Hornets, they had an event last week and I saw your girl."

By the way she rolled her eyes, I knew exactly who she was talking about. One day I was gonna get she and Dani to sit down and hash out whatever their issue is, but for now I would have to put up with their constant shade.

I sighed, "I hope you and Dani acted like ya'll had some sense."

"It was cool, she was with her man," She replied. "It didn't stop her from telling me about myself though. I was at work, so I couldn't get at her like I wanted to."

"I don't know why it has to be that way with ya'll."

"Look Tae, I know that's your girl but I think you need to watch yourself with her. She's coming for your club."

I laughed, "Dani doesn't even want to work there anymore. That's part of the reason we were arguing."

"You're laughing but I'm serious. She made sure to let me know that the club was hers and she wasn't going anywhere."

"I hear you Ang, but she was probably saying that

to get under your skin. That's just how she is, especially when she doesn't like you."

"Okay, you got it but when she tries to get you out of there, don't say I didn't warn you."

I thought back to the situation with Will the day before. He did tell me to watch out for my team, but I thought he was saying that just to fuck with me. Even still, the last person I ever thought he would be referring to was Dani. Sure, we'd been through some shit the past couple of months, but she would never do that to me. I wasn't going to change my opinion of her just because Angie said so, especially because she never really thought much of her to begin with.

After we finished lunch, Angie helped me take out my braids and wash my hair. It was a lot longer than I liked, but I would have to call Dani to give me a serious trim. For the time being, I blow dried and flat ironed it, and put it in a cute bun. After I got my hair together, I fed Somaiya, and let Angie hang out with her while I finished getting ready. I wasn't in the mood to cook again, so I ordered delivery from his favorite soul food spot. I had to dig deep for it, but I was able to find some lingerie that didn't make me huge. My snapback after having Somaiya wasn't happening as fast as I would like it to, but I low key liked the weight I was currently at. Except for my stomach, my curves were popping. The last thing I was able to do before Angie left, was grab some wine from the liquor store. We were completely out of wine, and I needed a serious drink with everything that I had going on.

Once Angie left, I put the baby to bed around nine and waited for him in the living room. Trell said he would be home around ten thirty, but it after ten thirty came and gone, I started to get upset. He had me sitting so long that I ended up drifting off to sleep. I didn't even realize it until I woke up and looked at the time. I was so irritated with him; he'd been so unreliable lately. Not only did he tell me that he would be home two hours ago, but he kept sending me to voicemail every time I called. I was about to call the police until I heard a car pull up in the driveway. I ran to open the door, and immediately got pissed off when I saw Trell's friend Jackson get out of the car.

"What's going on? I asked.

"He had a few too many," He replied. "I'm trying to get him out of the car."

I sighed, and slammed the door. I couldn't believe this bullshit. Here I was feeling bad because I hadn't been making time for him, and he's out getting wasted with his friends. I went upstairs to grab some shoes, and went back downstairs to open the garage. I walked out to Trell's car, where Jackson was still trying to get him to get out.

"La' Trell, get the fuck out of this car!" I yelled.

"Taela, I love you," he said, slurring his words.

I felt myself starting to tear up, and Jackson could sense that I was getting upset as well.

"Tae, just go inside with Somaiya. I'll make sure he gets in okay."

"Thank you. You can put him on the couch, I'll get him from there."

I went back inside, and went straight to Somaiya's room to check on her. She was on her way to sleep, so I left her in her bed. I went into the guest room, and got the bed ready for Trell. He knew the drill just as well as I did. If you come in this house drunk, you will be sleeping alone. I felt like I shouldn't have to set that type of boundary with him, but it is what it is. Not to say I didn't understand why he got in his feelings every once in a while, especially with today being Boo's birthday. Still this shit was getting out of hand, and something was going to have to change immediately.

I went back downstairs, to check on Jackson and Trell, and was surprised to see them sitting on my couch.

"Thank you for bringing him home," I said.

"You know I got my boy, I just hate to see him like this." He replied.

"Yeah, it's not the easiest thing in the world, but I don't know what to do about him."

"Just be there for him," he said. "I don't think any of us really know how much Boo's death still affects him. Clearly, he has some shit to work through. He only does this when he's upset about him."

This wasn't new to me, but to hear it confirmed by someone he respected meant a lot. I needed to get him help, which I knew would be a task.

"Thanks Jackson," I said, hugging him.

He left, and I sat on the couch next to Trell. He was knocked out, so I decided not to take him upstairs. I covered him with a blanket, and started up the stairs.

"You not gonna take me upstairs?" I hears him ask.

I rolled my eyes and went back into the living room.

I sighed, "La' Trell, you need to sleep this shit off

down here. I'll come check on you in the morning."

"I wanna say good night to my baby." He slurred.

"She's sleeping, and you don't need to wake her up. You can see her in the morning."

He stood up with his legs wobbling, and walked towards me.

"I'm going to see my daughter." He said, trying to put some bass in his voice.

He stumbled past me and started to go upstairs, but I was able to push him out of my way. I ran to baby girl's room, and took her into our room making sure to lock the door behind me. Trell started knocking on the door, but from the sound of it, he was on the floor. This fool must've crawled up the stairs.

"Crawl your ass to the guest room, and sleep there!" I yelled. "You're not coming in here."

I almost forgot that I had a sleeping baby lying next to me. I hadn't, waken her up, but if I kept on with her father, it would only be a matter of time.

"Tae! Let me in our room," he called out.

"You gotta go Trell, I can't be with you while you're like this."

"I just want to sleep with my family."

I ignored him and turned on the white noise

machine that I used to help Somaiya sleep. As I dozed of to sleep with tears in my eyes, Trell's knocks turned into scratches and then eventually they stopped.

I woke up the next morning, and immediately opened the bedroom door. Trell was still laying there, knocked out. I lightly kicked him to wake him up. He looked up at me with crust in his eyes, and I almost cried because I didn't recognize this person. It killed me to see him going through whatever he was going through, but I this was unacceptable.

"Get up and get in the shower, Trell." I said.

"Babe I'm–"

"Don't even," I said cutting him off. "Get in the shower, and then come downstairs so we can talk."

I helped him off the floor, and he went to get in the shower. I took baby girl downstairs so I could feed her, and put her in her jumper. I laughed watching her get excited about jumping. She had the most infectious laugh. There was no way anyone could hear it and not smile. That was something she got from her father. He could make anyone laugh at his jokes, not because he was funny, but because his laugh was so funny it made you laugh. Another thing I loved about him. Remembering those things and seeing them in our daughter was getting us through right now. I knew that he was a good man, but we needed to get back to a good place.

When Trell came downstairs, he walked in the living room like a child who knew they were in trouble. He sat next to me on the couch, and stared at me, waiting me to chew him out. I stayed silent, and kept watching Somaiya play with the toys on her jumper.

"I guess you want me to say something." He said.

"What I want is for you not to come in here like that."

"I know it was a lot."

"It was more than a lot La' Trell, it was fucking ridiculous." I said. " You need to quit the drinking, or you cannot live here. I will not let my daughter grow up with a drunk for a daddy."

"So now I'm a drunk?"

"If you keep on down this road, you will be. I get that you're upset about Boo, but you can't do what you did last night."

"I don't know what to do Tae. I haven't been able to shake that shit."

"You need to go to therapy and talk about it."

"I don't know about all of that Tae."

"Trell you're depressed and it's causing you to drink."

"So we can talk about my depression, but not yours?"

I had to laugh. Of course he would try to turn this around on me, and clearly he's been talking to my mother. She'd been constantly ranting about postpartum depression, so I knew it was only a matter of time before someone else came at me with it. Still I knew that if I was going to get him to go to a therapist, I would go just to shut him up.

"Look, if you think I need to go talk to someone, I will. Just know that if you don't go, you will be moving out of here."

"I promise you I'll do anything to keep my family together."

He leaned over and kissed me on the forehead. Any other time, that was enough reassurance that everything would be okay. Sadly, I wasn't so sure about it this time. All I could do was keep my end of our bargain and see what happens.

## CHAPTER 12

Even though I was off for the day, I still needed to pay the bills for the club. Trell ran out to the store once he sobered up , so that was the perfect time to get some work done. I logged onto my office computer and started to pay the gas and electric bill, but for some reason the card declined.

"Oh hell no," I said aloud.

I quickly grabbed my phone and logged into the banking app for the club. There was money in the savings account, but there wasn't enough to cover the whole light bill in the checking. I logged out of the app and called Dani.

"Hello," she answered on the first ring.

"Hey D," I greeted. "Did you pull the money from last week from the safe?"

"I gave it to Envy last night so she could make the

deposit this morning. Why?"

"I went to pay the light bill and it wasn't in the account."

"I'll call her and see what's happening."

"Can you do it on three way please?"

"Got it," Dani said before clicking over.

After about thirty seconds, Dani clicked back over and the other line was ringing.

"Hello," A man's voice answered.

"Hi is this Ramon?" Dani asked.

"Yeah, wassup Dani."

"I got Tae on the line and we really need to speak to Envy right now."

"She's talking to the doctor right now," he said. "That's why I have her phone."

"Doctor?" I replied.

"She didn't text ya'll last night?"

"No, she didn't," Dani said. "We were calling because she didn't make the bank deposit for the club this morning."

Ramon sighed, "On her way home, she got stopped by someone pretending to be the cops and the robbed her. They beat her up pretty bad."

"Are you serious?"

"I would've called ya'll if I'd known she didn't send the text. I don't know who did this, but when I found out, it's over.

"Oh shit, we're on our way." I replied.

"Can ya'll meet us at her spot, we'll be leaving here soon."

"We'll see ya'll there." Dani said before disconnecting from Ramon.

"Do you need me to swing by and come get you?" She asked.

"Nah, I'll meet you there." I replied. "I gotta wait for Trell to come home from the store before I go."

"Is he gonna be okay with you leaving?"

"I don't see why he wouldn't be. This is serious."

"Okay then, I'll see you at Envy's."

We hung up the phone and I tried to process everything. It seemed as if no matter what I did, whoever was behind this seemed to inch closer and closer to me. A security guard and a bottle girl was one thing, but now he was coming for my managers. Whoever it was, they had been well informed about my operations within the club. It made me think that maybe that clown Will wasn't lying when he told me to look at my people on the inside. Someone had to know that Envy was the one who made the deposits. Although I initially ruled Dani out of any conversation about disloyalty, I couldn't help but think that she was one of the few who knew. I would definitely have to get to the bottom of this. When Trell came back from the store, I was a little nervous to tell him that I was running off yet again. He completely understood, and I was happy it wasn't causing an issue. Envy was more than just an employee, she was a good friend and I needed to be there for her.

A rushed over to Envy's house, not knowing how to feel. I was worried about Envy, worried about the club, and most of all worried about my family. I was also a bit paranoid driving over there. This could've been the robber's plan the whole time in order to get to me. If they knew as much as they seemed to, then they knew I would come running if my girl got hurt.

When I got to Envy's, I took a deep breath before going inside. I was trying to keep it together, but I honestly felt like shit. Everything that is happening is a result of my screw up, and I needed it all to stop.

As I approached, I saw that Envy's door was open, so I tapped on her screen door.

"Hello!" I called out.

Ramon came to unlock the screen door, and let me in.

"They're in Envy's room," He informed.

I went up to Envy's room, where she and Dani were kicking it on her bed.

"Hey honey," I greeted. "How are you feeling?"

"I'm sore and my body hurts, but nothing too serious," she replied. "I made it out with only two cracked ribs, so I'm good."

"What the hell happened, E?" Dani asked.

"I was driving home and a car pulled up behind me. I didn't think anything of until they started flashing police lights. When I pulled over a man in black rushed to the car demanding that I give him the money," she explained. "When I told him no, he pulled me out the car and started hitting me. Then he took the money from under my seat."

Envy stopped talking and started to tear up. I felt for her, and wished that she never got caught up in my mess.

"I'm sorry that happened to you Envy." I sympathized.

Dani was on the edge of the bed in tears, and all I could keep thinking about was what Will told me.

"Look, I'll work off what he took," she said. "Just give me a day or two and I'll be back to work."

"Take as much time as you need before you come back to work, your safety is important." I replied.

"Tae, you need to be careful," she warned. "He said that you needed to watch your back."

I sighed. I knew it was coming, but not this soon. Hearing it from Envy made it real to me, and it was really messing with me.

"I'll be okay, E."

"I don't trust that," Dani replied. "We need to go to the police."

"I don't trust them."

Dani looked as if she was going to say something, but instead she just shook her head. I wasn't going to sit and argue with her. I didn't need to. I said I wasn't calling the police and that was that.

"I know you think you're superwoman Tae, but I really want you to watch out." Envy said.

"I got you," I replied. "I'll get Kylan to put in some extra hours just to be safe."

I reached down to hug Envy, and kept the conversation going. I was dreading the moment we left, because I knew D would start with her nagging.

Fortunately, we were there for a good two hours before Envy started to nod off from her pain meds. I was hoping that Dani would just drop the subject, but of course she didn't. As soon as we left the house she started.

"Tae I don't know what you're doing but you need to stop." She whispered with aggression.

"What are you talking about?" I replied sarcastically.

"You need the call the police and tell them what Envy told you. This is getting out of hand."

"Why call them, when I can handle it myself."

She sighed, "Handle it how."

I didn't say anything, but Dani caught my drift. She stepped back from me and shook her head in disbelief.

"Tae I don't know who the hell you think you are, but this isn't a damn movie." She started whispering again, "You got away with Shaun and King, but don't you think your luck is going to run out at some point?"

"Danita, chill out. I'm gonna handle this my way."

"Whatever," she said. "Just remember that you're not the only one who's being affected by this. Envy was laid up in a hospital bed all night!"

"Are you saying this is my fault?"

"No, but if someone else gets hurt it will be." She said before storming off to her car.

I wanted to be upset with her, but she was right. All of this was my fault and I'd been putting my staff in danger trying to prove myself. Still I wasn't about to let anyone punk me. So I texted Kylan, and told him to meet me at the club. It was time to end this shit for good, and I didn't care who I needed to take out. The first thing I needed to do was figure out who was working for the enemy, then I had to figure out who the enemy was. My only ear to the streets out her was Kylan, so we would have to do it together.

When I pulled up to the club, I instantly got irritated when I saw Aylin standing outside. I wasn't in the mood to deal with her today, and if she came on some bullshit she would quickly regret it.

"Don't you have some chirping to do somewhere else, bird?" I asked.

Aylin smirked, "Aren't you happy to see me?"

"I got too much going on to deal with you. So please take your ass on before I have to put my hands on you."

"You may wanna hold off on that."

I sighed, "Why is that?"

Aylin reached into her purse and tossed a small piece of paper at me. I started to lunge at her until I realized what it was, a sonogram. I picked it up off the ground and stared at it. I was speechless.

"What's wrong, sis?" she taunted. "Don't you wanna congratulate me? Somaiya's gonna be a big sister."

In that moment, I didn't know what to do. I wanted to swing on her so bad, but I couldn't hit a pregnant woman. I wanted to break down, but I would never give her the satisfaction. So I went with option three, which was to leave that hoe standing there and take my ass home to lay La' Trell out.

# CHAPTER 13

I was so pissed by the time I got home, that I almost kicked the door in. My uncle, who was chilling in my living room, hopped up when he hear the front door fly open.

"Taela what the hell, I thought you were someone trying to break in here." He said, trying to catch his breath.

I wasn't even trying to hear whatever he was saying. I had more important shit to tend to.

"La' Trell!" I called up the stairs. "Trell, get your ass down here!"

Trell came running down the stairs. He couldn't get a word out before I started swinging on him. He started blocking my punches, which pissed me off even more, so I started going harder. He blocked what he could until he was able to grab a hold of my wrists and restrain me.

"Taela I love you, but you need to chill with all that hitting bullshit," he said, firmly.

I was pissed off at him, but I was no fool. I didn't think that he would purposely hit me, but there is only so much a man can take before his reflexes kick in. I stopped putting up a fight so he would let me go, and when he did I broke down. He looked at me with a confused look.

"Taela, what the hell is going on?" he asked

"After everything that you know that I've been through, why would you get this bitch pregnant?" I said through tears.

"What are you talking about?"

I reached in my back pocket and handed him the ultrasound. He gave a frustrated sigh as he looked at it.

"Come on Tae, I know you don't believe this shit. I haven't spoken to this girl, let alone slept with her ass."

"I just want to know why you would do this to me, Trell?"

Trell tried to grab my hand, but I snatched it from him.

"I don't know why you're letting her get in your head, but I didn't touch that girl."

"How the hell do you know? The past couple of months you've been drunk out of your damn mind!"

"Knock it off Tae," he said. "I have never been so drunk that I wouldn't remember sleeping with someone."

"Look, you need to go stay with your mom tonight, and you can get the rest of your stuff tomorrow."

"I'll sleep in the guest room, but I'm not leaving this house." He replied.

I didn't know if he thought I was playing, but I was beyond serious. I went into the kitchen, and went straight to our knife set that was on top of the counter. Trell, who was trailing behind me, stopped when I grabbed the paring knife and threw it at him. He was luck my aim was off, because if he had been two inches to the left, I would've grazed his cheek.

"You can stand there if you want, but I promise you that I'm not gonna miss every time." I threatened.

Trell shook his head, "Clearly, you've lost your damn mind, so I'm out. I'll be back in the morning to see Somaiya."

He dragged his sorry ass out the front door. I didn't

know if he was going to his mother's, or to be with his bum ass baby mama, but he was no longer my problem. I would be sure to send his ring back, because I didn't even want the shit anymore. He could continue to be a father to Somaiya but he and I were done for good.

Once I calmed down and became aware of my surroundings, I noticed Somaiya was crying. Uncle Leon was no longer in the living room, so I figured he was up there with her. I felt a little lightheaded, but I still wanted to see what was going on with my baby. The last thing I remembered was going up the first set of stairs before everything went black.

****************************

I opened my eyes and was in a state of confusion. I felt like I had been hit by a truck, and I was in the hospital with an IV in my arm. My mom sitting next to my bed on the phone, and Dani was sitting on the sofa in the room reading. I quickly sat up to get a better look at the room.

"Why am I here?" I asked.

Dani came over to the bed as my mother finished up her phone call. Dani gave me a super long hug.

"Dani, what happened?" I asked again.

"Apparently you passed out on your stairs, and Jacqueline found you."

Before I could get out my next question, my mom rushed over.

"You scared the hell out of me, Taela." She said.

"I know, Ma. I don't remember what happened."

"The doctor said you passed out from stress." She said. "It's probably because you went back to work so early."

"I don't think that has anything to do with it. I just have a lot of other things going on." I replied. "Where is Somaiya?"

"Your uncle has her. I tried to call Trell but his phone was off."

"I'm not really worried about Trell right now." I replied. "Can you call Uncle Leon and tell him to bring her up here?"

"Sure," my mother replied, before stepping out of the room.

I looked at Dani and started tearing up. I didn't want to tell her about Aylin, but I had to get the shit out.

"D, shit is bad. Trell got the bitch Aylin pregnant." I blurted out.

"Shorty from the boutique?" she asked. "What the hell?"

"On my way home from Envy's I stopped at the club, and she was waiting outside to hand me a sonogram."

Dani took a hard sigh. I could tell she was trying to figure out the right thing to say, but I wasn't sure that there was a right thing.

"You know that hoe is just doing that to break ya'll up. Trell would never do that to you." She said.

"Dani, this isn't the first time she's approached me about him," I explained. "We haven't been speaking, so I haven't been able to fill you in. Trell has been drinking a lot and he ran into her at a bar about three or four months ago."

"What is he saying about this?"

"He swears he never touched her, and that he's never gotten so drunk that he blacks out. I just don't know what to believe."

"I can't tell you what to do, but I can tell you that Trell loves you to death. I don't believe for one second that he slept with that girl."

"If it were you and Jonathan, what would you do?"

I watched as Dani thought about her response. .It

was always easy for people to give advice about these situations when they're not in it.

"Well, I would at least talk to him." She finally responded. "Anyone can make some shit up, and he deserves a chance to make his case."

"Dani, I just don't know if I can do that right now." I replied.

"Do you, boo. Ii just don't want you to regret it later."

I knew she was right, but I really didn't want to hear anything he had to say. I needed a few days to deal with everything, and if I let him come home, I'd be angry all over again. I refused to keep going through this shit with him. Either we were going to be together and do right by each other, or we needed to go our separate ways. I couldn't keep stressing about him. It was literally tearing me apart.

As Dani was about to speak again, my mother came back in the room with the doctor. Dani resumed her seat on the other side of the room, and left me to speak with the doctor.

"How are you feeling Miss McCray? I'm Dr. Williams." She greeted.

"I feel like I got hit by a truck." I replied.

"Well from what your mother told me, you took a pretty long fall so that's expected."

"'Is everything going to be okay?" I asked.

"You'll be fine. You just need to take it easy."

"Thanks doctor, I'll get on it."

"I'll start getting you discharged," she said before leaving the room.

I was happy to hear that I was getting out of there. I had too much shit going on to be confined to hospital bed, and I missed my daughter.

"Did you get in touch with Uncle Leon?" I asked my mother.

"Yes, he said everything is fine, but I told him not to come." She said, "I figured you would be getting discharged soon."

"That's fine."

"Where is Trell?" she asked.

I ignored her, and started getting ready to leave.

"Danita, can you bring my clothes over here so I can start getting dressed?" I asked.

She caught the hint and went to sit down by the window. I didn't want to talk about it, especially not with her. I needed to figure out what was going to happen with us before I started talking to a bunch of people about it.

Luckily, it wasn't too much longer until the nurses got me discharged. I wasn't feeling one hundred percent, but I was glad to be out of there. I couldn't wait to be in my own bed, cuddling up with my daughter. It seemed like she was the only one that I had in my corner.

As my mother and I rode home in silence, I thought about my next course of action. I agreed with Dani about talking to Trell, and I would in due time. The thought of him not being home felt crazy. I knew that this was the way it had to be until I got to the bottom of this, and I was determined to do so. However before I said anything to him, I wanted to speak to Aylin's hoe ass.

When I got home, I plopped down on the couch and took in the emptiness. I never thought that I would be living here alone. All I could do was shake my head.

"Are you okay Taela?" My mother asked.

"I'm fine, I was just thinking," I replied. "Can you go get lil mama for me?"

"Sure," she said before going up the stairs.

As soon as she was out of earshot, I called Kylan. It

was late in the afternoon so I knew he would be out.

"Hey boss," he answered. "How are you feeling?"

"I'm good Ky, but this is not a friendly call," I replied. "I need you to get an address for me."

"Okay cool, whose address do you need?"

"Do you remember when you came in to the club a while back, and me and a girl were getting into it?"

"Yeah I remember."

"Her name is Aylin and she works in a boutique called Bella," I explained. "It's around the corner from the club."

"I'm on it. Just send me a picture of shorty, and I'll figure it out."

I wanted to give Ky more details but I heard someone coming down the stairs. The last thing I needed was for someone to hear what I was plotting.

"Thanks Ky, I gotta go." I said before quickly hanging up.

Uncle Leon came down the stairs shaking his head.

"I see you're still on your shit." He said.

"What are you talking about?" I asked.

He chuckled, "I'll play this game with you for now. Just don't call me when whatever you're doing goes south."

I sighed as he went out the front door. As soon as I handled this shit with Aylin, I was done with all the drama. I had some rebuilding to do, and I didn't need anything messing with my focus.

# CHAPTER 14

It only took three days of Trell not being home, for me to lose my mind. It was okay at first because my mom was here to help out, but once she left, it was a struggle. Trying to work, and manage everything at home was no joke. It made me appreciate my mother for everything she did for me, especially when I was younger. She practically raised me by herself, with no help after my father passed. I was happy that Trell came to take her in the evenings so I could go into the club. Since we were only seeing each other in passing, we still hadn't had a conversation, but that was mainly because every time I saw him, I got mad all over again. I was also waiting to have my talk with Aylin.

Kylan texted me earlier to tell me that he got Aylin's address, so instead of going to the club this evening, I was gonna pull up on her. I had too many of questions that needed answers. I tried to call Angie to see if she wanted to ride with me to Aylin's. It had been a minute since I last saw her, and I was a little worried. I knew that she was doing work down here, but usually she would've called or come over by now. Unfortunately, she didn't pick up the phone, so I called Dani. Even if she wasn't down to ride with me, I knew she would tell me what I needed to hear.

"Hey girl, what's happening?" Dani answered.

"D, I need your help." I said. "I'm about to pull up on Aylin."

"Taela, why are you doing this?"

"I need to talk to her," I said. "I need answers."

"Get your answers from Trell."

"I don't know if I can trust him right now."

"So you trust her?" She asked. "You need to talk to your man, and leave that hoe right where she is."

"Look, I need to do this for my piece of mind. Can you come with me?"

She sighed, "What time are you trying to go over there?"

"I told Trell to be here by six, so I can come get you once he comes."

"That's cool, but I'll swing by to get you. I wanna

see my god daughter before we go."

"I'm with it. I'll see you later."

"Bet," She said before ending the call.

I tried to make myself busy, so I wouldn't think about what could possibly go down with Aylin. While I wanted to believe that Trell wouldn't cheat on me, I didn't want to be naive. I just needed to know for my own sanity. The worst case scenario was that she confirm everything she was saying from the jump. Either way, I just needed to brace myself for whatever was going to happen.

Dani got to the house around five, and went straight to Somaiya's room. It's crazy how once you have a baby nobody wants to see you anymore. It's always about the little one. I couldn't blame them though because Lil Mama was amazing.

I let Dani have her time with Somaiya while I cleaned up the house. It was the first time I'd had a free moment to myself to get some housework done. As I was washing the dishes, I heard the garage opening. Assuming it was my Uncle coming to check on us, I didn't think anything of it. However, I got a huge surprise when I saw Trell come in the garage entrance with a large bouquet of flowers. He was trying so hard, and I wasn't moved at all. I just rolled my eyes and went back to washing the dishes.

"Hello Taela," He said.

"Hi La' Trell, Somaiya is upstairs with Dani." I replied.

He sat the flowers down on the counter, and sat at the island.

"Can we talk about this?" he asked.

I sighed, "The only thing we need to talk about is our daughter."

"Tae, I don't know what I need to do to get you to believe me. I never slept with Aylin."

"To be honest, I don't know either. Just give me some time."

He stood up with a defeated look on his face, and went upstairs. I knew that wasn't the response he was looking for, but it was all that I had to give. I wished that I had a real answer for him. I was so torn, and I didn't really know what I wanted or needed from him in this moment. All I wanted was for this to never have happened in the first place. Of course, I couldn't go back in time, but I still didn't know how to move forward.

After a minute or two, Dani came bouncing down

the stairs. I knew she would want to know what just went down with Trell, but I didn't want to talk about it. It seemed like lately that was how I coped with my problems. It's a terrible habit that I've developed, especially because the only time I let that shit out was when I was pulling a trigger. Nonetheless, the only thing I wanted to talk about at the moment, was what I had to say to Aylin. It was going to take everything in me not to put hands on her since she's pregnant, but that was partly why I was glad Dani was coming. She wouldn't let me get too worked up.

The whole ride to the house I kept imagining scenarios in my mind. This was something I never thought I would have to do, and yet here I am. All I could do right now was hope for the best. Although right now I couldn't tell what that was.

When the GPS let us know that the destination was coming up on the right, my stomach started doing flips. Noticing that I was starting to panic, Dani pulled over.

"Tae, we can go back home," she said. "All you have to do is say the word."

All I could say was "No, drive."

Dani started driving again, and finally the GPS

informed us that we had arrived. Surprisingly, we weren't the only visitors she had. My jaw dropped when I saw a black Rav-4 with Maryland tags parked on Aylin's parking pad.

"What the hell?" I said aloud.

"What happened?" Dani asked.

"That's my sister's car."

"It could be a coincidence."

"I'm about to find out," I said

I took out my phone and found Angie's contact. I dialed the number and put her on speaker so Dani could hear. The phone rang longer than it usually did before she picked up.

"Hey sis, what's going on?" She answered.

"Hey, are you busy right now?" I asked.

"Nah, I'm in my Air bnb working on a few things."

I looked at Dani and shook my head.

"Really?" I replied. "I'm outside right now and I don't see your car."

"I meant that I'm almost there," she lied. "I'll be back in about ten minutes, if you want to wait."

Before I could say a word, Angie rushed out of Aylin's house and got in her car. Dani's jaw dropped in disbelief.

"Nah, it's okay," I said. "I'll just go home."

"I'm sorry sis, let's plan to meet up in a few days." She said.

"Sure," I replied before hanging up.

As much as I tried not to, I couldn't stop the tears from falling. Everyone was right about her, and it pissed me off.

"I was never a huge fan of the girl, but I never thought she would do something like this." Dani said.

"I don't even know what to think right now." I replied

"Tae, I'm sorry."

"Can you take me home please?" I asked.

Dani drove off, and we rode home in silence. I didn't have anything to say, and at this point I didn't know what to think. I hated to think that my own sister was in cahoots with the bitch who was trying to tear my family apart, but right now, that's what it looked like. When we pulled in my driveway, I was trying to make sense of this. Nothing seemed right about this, and I felt myself starting to lose it. In times like these, there was only one person I could call. Even though we weren't seeing eye to eye right now, I knew that he would give me the real. so I swallowed my pride and called him.

"Hey baby girl," he answered.

"Uncle Leon, shit is crazy right now." I replied.

"What's up?"

"I know Trell told you what was going on with us."

"Yes, he's been staying with me."

I was a little shocked to hear that. I knew that they'd been getting close, but I didn't know it was like that. As refreshing as that was to hear, I couldn't think about that right now.

"So, I went to confront the girl, and Angie was there."

Uncle Leon sighed, "Did you physically see her?"

"At first I just saw her car," I explained. "Then I called her and not only did she lie about where she was, but she got in her car and drove off because she thought I was at her place."

"Do you think she's behind all of the craziness at the club?"

"If I had to guess, I would say yes."

Uncle Leon went silent. I knew his wheels were turning, and I needed him to make sense of all of this.

"So, what should I do?" I asked.

"At this point you need to know what you're up

against," he said. "Start talking to this Aylin chick. Since she's pregnant you'll be able to get answers out of her the easiest."

"What about Angie?"

"If she set this shit up, then she could possibly be more dangerous than we think. Let me deal with her. Just keep your phone by you."

"Will do," I said.

"One more thing Taela," he said before I could hang up.

"Yes?"

"Let that man come home," he said. "He looks pitiful sleeping on my damn couch."

I smiled and gave a light chuckle.

"I'll think about it," I replied.

I hung up the phone, and hugged Dani. I loved her for once again riding with me through some craziness. When Angie came out of that house she could've hit me with 'I told you so', but she didn't. She was there for me despite what we'd been going through the past few weeks, and that was exactly what I needed.

"Thanks, D. I'll call you later." I said.

"If you want me to go with you to talk to Aylin for real, I'm down," she replied. "Just give it a few days."

"I will. I need to relax and spend some time with my daughter."

I hopped out of Dani's car and slowly walked into my garage. I was emotionally and physically drained at this point, and I needed to lie down. I made my way to the living room to lay on the couch, but Trell was already there. Not wanting to wake him, I tried to turn and go upstairs, but he heard me.

"Hey, did you just get back?" he asked groggily.

"Yeah, I'm back." I replied.

"Since I have you here, can we finally talk?"

"Trell, I don't have it in me to argue with you, so say whatever it is that you have to say."

"Tae, I need you to hear me when I say that I never touched that girl," he pleaded. "We can go talk to her if you want."

I laughed quietly, "I actually just came from there."

Trell sat all the way up.

"So what did she say," he inquired.

"I never got to talk to her," I explained. "Dani and I pulled up and saw Angie's car in the driveway. They're up to something, but I don't know what it is."

"Damn, this doesn't make sense."

"Yeah, I know."

"Look, I get that you're upset with me right now, but I'm not going to let you stay in this house alone."

"I'm fine La' Trell." I argued.

"Tae when I put that ring on your finger, that was my promise to protect you and our daughter," he reasoned. "I don't care how much you try to fight it. I'm coming home."

The stubbornness in me wanted to resist, but I couldn't deny that I felt much safer with him around. Even though things weren't completely right with us right now, I knew that I needed him here with me. So I quit the tough girl act, sat next to him and laid my head on his chest. Knowing that I could always be loving and soft with him was extremely soothing. I had to get it out while I could, because as soon as I stepped foot out of this house I knew that all that soft shit would have to be tucked away.

# CHAPTER 15

I had no desire to leave my house after finding out my sister was a snake. Everything I needed was with me at home. Usually I'd be itching to get back to work, but at this point, I'd taken four days off and I didn't care. The crazy thing was, I didn't see myself going back in to work for at least another two or three days. Per usual, Dani held down everything at the club, and Envy had returned to work. It finally felt like my support system was back intact. Trell and I were still working through the situation with Aylin, and Uncle Leon was working day and night to get the low down on Angie. I was happy about that because I didn't have the mental capacity to play detective right now.

During my time off, Trell and I had some time to sort through our relationship. He still insisted that he never touched Aylin, and I decided to take him at his word. He'd never lied to me before, and I didn't have a real reason not to believe him. All I had was Aylin's word, and knowing what I know now, this could all be a part of whatever she and Angie were cooking up. Still, it would take some time to rebuild the trust between us, but we were willing to put in the work. We also made appointments for individual and couples therapy, so we were on the right track to getting where we needed to be.

Either way, I was making the best out of my time away from the outside world. Angie had been calling me nonstop since I caught her at Aylin's house. Since Uncle Leon was doing what he did best, I decided distance myself. That was hard as shit, since I'm never the one to bite my tongue when I'm upset.

My phone started ringing, and I rolled my eyes when I saw Angie's name pop up. Everything in me wanted to pick up the phone and lay her ass out, but I just ignored it.

"Was that your sister again?" Trell asked from the kitchen.

"Yeah, it was her," I answered. "I wish she would stop calling me."

"Just put your phone on do not disturb."

"I can't, I need it on just in case Dani calls.

I was really waiting on my uncle to call, but I didn't want to tell him about it. I didn't want him trying to intervene. I was sick of everyone thinking they needed to fix my problems for me. I'd more than proven that I was perfectly capable of handling my own shit. I was only letting my uncle help me, because this was family business. Otherwise, I would've called Kylan.

I went on with the rest of the day as normal, and even took the time to cook dinner. I had been slacking recently, mostly because Trell's hungry ass hadn't been here. Tonight I made crab cakes, roasted potatoes, and steamed broccoli. It had been a minute since I had some authentic Maryland crab cakes, and it was one of the things I missed about being back home. It took me back to senior year, when Dani and I would skip school and sneak off to Baltimore to get one. I thought it would be nice to treat Trell to something I missed from back home. Once I set the table and fixed plates, I called Trell down to eat.

"Damn baby, you weren't playing when you said you missed cooking." He said, as he surveyed the table.

"Not at all," I responded. "I also have a pound cake

in the oven for dessert."

"Well let me sit down, so I can start working on this plate." He said.

We both sat down, but before I could take a bite of my food, my phone started ringing from the living room. Trell was visibly annoyed as he went to grab my phone for me. His face quickly changed when he saw the name on the phone.

"It's your uncle." He stated.

I took my phone and quickly answered before it stopped ringing.

"Hey Uncle Leon, what's up?"

"Come take a ride with me." He replied.

"We're having dinner right now," I explained. "Can you come in like an hour?"

"I wasn't asking you," he said. "Put on some dark clothing and sneakers, and I'll be outside waiting for you."

Uncle Leon hung up the phone without waiting for a response. It really didn't seem like I had a choice in the matter, so I started wrapping up my plate.

"What's going on?" Trell questioned.

"I gotta ride somewhere with my uncle," I responded. "I'll be back in an hour."

I ran upstairs and put on an all-black Nike sweat suit and my black air maxes. I quickly gelled my hair down, and put in a cheap pair of studs that I got from the hair store. After checking my appearance to make sure I was looking good, I grabbed my gun and hurried outside.

"What's going on?" I asked reluctantly.

"Shhhh, listen," he instructed.

At first it was silent, but then I heard something bumping around in the back. It sounded like we were hitting speed bumps, but since we were parked in my driveway I knew that was ruled out.

"What the hell is that?" I asked.

Uncle Leon chuckled, "It's your sister."

My jaw dropped. I knew he worked fast, but I didn't know it would be that fast. I damn sure didn't expect her to be rolling around in his trunk

"Why are you like this?"

"Look, you called me for help. So let me help.

"Just get out of my driveway before one of my neighbors walk by," I instructed.

He quickly pulled out of my drive way, sped out of the neighborhood.

"So what's the plan?" I asked.

"We're going to end this, once and for all." He said, "Whatever you've been doing hasn't been working, and you can't keep living like this Tae."

I sucked my teeth, "How are you going to do that?"

"You'll find out when we get to our destination," he answered.

"Where exactly would that be?"

He griped, "Stop asking questions. The less you know the better."

I rolled my eyes. He had so much to say about how I handle my issues, but it didn't seem like he was any better than I was. On top of that, I hated how cryptic he was being. It made me feel like he didn't trust me. If anything, I was probably the most trustworthy person around him except for Tony. Nonetheless, it was clear that my uncle wasn't going to tell me the plan, so I changed the subject.

"Since I can't know what the plan is, can I at least know what you found out?"

He sighed, "Can't you just take a damn nap?"

"No at all," I shot back.

He rubbed his temple with his free hand. I was getting on his nerves, but I had a right to know what the hell was going on.

"On the day of your gender reveal, a black Rav-4 was sitting outside watching the house," he explained. "I had my suspicions when I saw Angie's car for the first time, but now I know it was her."

"So what are you saying?"

"I'm saying that Angie is behind the murders at your club."

"How do you know that?"

"That's all I'm going to tell you. She's gonna tell you the rest," he said. "Now please take a nap, and let me drive in silence."

I knew I wasn't going to be able to sleep with what he just told me, but I stopped asking him questions. I knew that when I was in savage mode, I didn't want to have any type of conversation. Considering that he just kidnapped my fraud ass sister, I realized that now was not the time to force information out of him.

As we continued to drive, I noticed a sign that said 'Welcome to South Carolina'. I didn't know where he was taking us, but I knew we were a good ways from home. When we got off the highway, all I saw was woods and darkness. Wherever we were, they didn't believe in street lights.

"Where are we?" I asked.

"Clover, South Carolina" He replied.

After about ten minutes, he turned on to an old dirt road that led up to an old farmhouse. He parked out front, and his friend Tony and another guy, came to get Angie from the trunk.

"What type of gangster movie shit are you on?" I asked jokingly.

"Don't question my methods," he replied. "I get the job done."

I followed my uncle into the house through the storm cellar. I could tell that the place had been abandoned, and probably hadn't had people inside of it for at least ten or fifteen years. When we got to the basement, they had Angie sitting on the floor, tied at her ankles and wrists and something covering her mouth. It was a hard sight to see, but I knew it had to be done.

"Uncover her mouth." My uncle instructed Tony.

As soon as Tony took the cover off Angie's mouth, she began gasping for air.

"What the fuck," she yelled in my uncle's direction. "What is going on?"

"You tell us." My uncle replied.

"Taela, what is going on?" Angie asked again.

"Ang, if you want to make it out of here alive, you need to tell us everything you did."

Uncle Leon gave me a side eye, but I didn't care. At the end of the day this was my sister, and if there was a chance that I could save her, I was going to do that.

"I don't know what you're talking about," she lied.

"I saw you coming out of Aylin's house." I said.

As soon as she heard Aylin's name, her eyes got big. She knew she'd been caught.

"Tae, I'm sorry. King told me everything before he left to come down here," she said. "He gave me instructions, and sent two of his goons down here. All of this was for him."

The whole time she was talking, I was fighting back tears.

"You killed innocent people who had nothing to do with the situation!" I yelled.

"You killed our brother!"

"No she killed her brother," Uncle Leon interjected.

I processed what Uncle Leon said, and felt my blood begin to boil.

"What do you mean by my brother?" I asked through clenched teeth.

A tear rolled down Angie's face.

"King got someone to fake the paternity test," she admitted.

I ran over to her and started kicking her. I wanted to punch that bitch in her face, but I still wasn't sure if she was gonna make it out of here alive. I didn't need my DNA winding up on her. Before I could do any real damage to her, Uncle Leon grabbed me.

"Tae, I'm sorry!" she screamed.

She could cry and scream all she wanted but I didn't give a damn. I let this bitch into my home, and around my family. I felt so betrayed, and at this point I was cool with never meeting any of my siblings. So far, I've met one that wanted to kill me, and another that turned out to be a complete fraud. I was done with her, but I knew she wasn't the only one involved in this plot. There was someone else that needed to be right here with her.

"Where's Aylin?" I asked my uncle.

"She left town last night. She's the one who told me about she and Angie's plan," he explained. "She also told me how they were able to pull it off."

Before he could keep explaining, we heard a car door slam. I looked at my uncle, and he nodded his head to let me know that everything was okay. My anxiety was off the charts as the person started to come down the stairs.

"Angie, why are there so many cars outside?" I heard a familiar voice ask.

I knew exactly who it was, but I needed to see her face before I could believe it was her.

# CHAPTER 16

Words couldn't describe the hurt I felt to see Envy standing at the bottom of those stairs. I still didn't what part she played in this, but the way she was avoiding eye contact with me said it all. As I started piecing things together in my mind, things started to make sense. The first time Aylin came into the club, they were arguing about something, and it didn't seem like it was their first time meeting. We used to see her all the time in the boutique, but they never spoke or gave any indication that they knew each other. I wasn't sure what Angie promised her, but it had to be a hell of a lot for her to turn on me like this. I just couldn't believe it.

"So this is for real Envy?" I asked. "You really set me up?"

"Tae, it was never supposed to go this far." She

replied.

"Well, damn how far was it supposed to go?"

"She was in it from the beginning," Angie said. "She was the only one who could help me get close enough to kill you."

My heart sank to my feet, and tears started to fall. We'd only been friends a short amount of time, but I never thought that she would be a part of this. I reached in my hoodie pocket and grabbed my gun. Envy started quivering.

"How much did she offer you?" I asked Envy,

"Tae, I'm s–"

"How much!" I yelled.

Envy broke down crying, "She was going to give me the money from the robbery."

I laughed in disbelief.

"That was you too?" I exclaimed. "Your stupid ass let someone beat on you for some money?"

"Tae, I promise I wasn't gonna let her kill you. I just needed the money." She pleaded.

"That's a lie," Angie interjected. "She wanted your club, and she even offered to take you out herself when you told her about the Atlanta spot."

"Shut the fuck up Angie, you're the one that got

the fake sonograms made!" Envy yelled.

"And you lured Gino to his house so Chaos could get to him."

At that point, I'd had enough. I didn't want to know anything else.

I shouted, "Both of you shut up!"

The two of them going back and forth was pissing me off even more. As far as I was concerned both of these bitches had to go, and I was done listening to them tell on each other. It was time to finish this shit.

"What do you want to do with Angie?" Uncle Leon asked.

As much as I hated the bitch, I couldn't kill her myself. The past few months I had gotten to know her as my blood, and even though she wasn't I still couldn't do it. On the other hand, I had no problem with someone else doing it.

"Get rid of her, but don't do it in here." I instructed.

Uncle Leon motioned for Tony to take Angie away. She started screaming and pleading for me to tell them to stop, but it wasn't gonna happen. Once they made it outside, I heard a single gunshot and the Angie's cries stopped. I looked at my uncle for confirmation that we were still good. I knew that we were basically in the middle of nowhere, but I wasn't sure if people were close enough to hear the gunshot.

"We're good," he assured.

"Good, because I need a minute with Envy," I replied.

He looked unsure at first, but then he reluctantly went outside. Envy watched him go up the stairs, and I could tell that she knew what was about to go down. There was absolutely no way out of it. Even if she tried to run, my uncle would catch her outside. There was only one way out of here for her, and that was through me.

"So this is where we are, huh?" she asked.

"Not for nothing, you plotted with a bitch to have me killed."

"Tae, I wasn't gonna let her do that to you. You gotta believe me."

"What the hell am I supposed to do with that, E?"

"I know you won't let me come back to work at the club, but I can start dancing again to pay you your money back."

"You think this is about the money?" I asked. "Dani and I took you in like family. You were going to be in my wedding!"

"I know, just let me make it up to you. I'm begging you."

I couldn't believe she actually thought that what she did was forgivable. People lost lives behind her participating in this bullshit.

"I just need to know, why would you let them take Terrell?"

Envy didn't respond, and started crying.

"Her daughter is going to grow up without her mother! Gino's kids are going to miss their father!" I yelled, as she sobbed harder. "Even if I did let you live, how the hell would that even work?"

"Tae, we can figure something out."

Deep down I wanted to believe that everything could go back to normal if I just erased her from my life, but I couldn't trust her. She'd taken too much from me already, and who's to say that she wouldn't try me again.

"I'm sorry it had to come to this, E." I said, "I love you and I always will, but you went too far."

I let off three shots in her chest, and froze. Shortly my uncle came down the storm cellar, and lightly kicked her limp body. Realizing she was dead, I started hyperventilating. Uncle Leon slowly walked over to me and reached for the gun, which was still pointed where Envy had been standing.

"I'm here Tae, just hand me the gun." He said.

I could hear him perfectly, but I was having a full on panic attack and couldn't move. The last time we went through this, I was curled up one the floor after killing Shaun.

"Give me the gun, Tae." He commanded.

I slowly lowered the gun into his hand.

"I'll bring you a new one tomorrow." He said.

"I don't want the shit back," I said. "I'm done."

"Go to the car, I'll be out in a minute." He said.

On my way to the car, I kept wishing that all of this was a dream. I hated who I'd become over the past few months. To some, I was just doing what I had to do, but I didn't want to have to keep doing this. I'd finally had enough. Once Tony and my uncle got Envy's body in Tony's truck, my uncle got in the car.

"Are you okay?" He asked.

"I'm fine, is everything cleaned up?"

"Yeah, it's good," he assured. "Let's get you home."

On the ride back to Charlotte, Uncle Leon kept trying to talk to me but I wasn't for it. We'd clearly switched places since the ride down. All I could think about was what I was going to do about Dani. I wanted to tell her what happened, but I wasn't sure how she would take the news of me killing Envy. I'd made a complete mess of things, and I wished that I listened to my uncle weeks ago. He warned me that shit would get real, and it definitely did. When we pulled up to my house, it was about four in the morning. My uncle parked in the driveway and sat as if he was waiting for me to get out.

"Are you not coming in?" I asked.

"Nah, I have something I need to do." He replied, "Plus, you're gonna need some sleep."

"Well, come by later. I made crab caked last night, so I'll reheat them for lunch."

"I'm not gonna make it," he said sadly.

I realized his eyes were watery.

"What's wrong?" I asked.

"Taela, I'm going to turn myself in."

I was so taken back by what he said that I couldn't speak for a minute. I knew what he was trying to do, but I couldn't let him.

"This is my fault," I said. "I need to own up to this shit. I'll turn myself in later today, but I need to say goodbye to my family first."

"You have your whole life ahead of you, baby girl. I've lived my life, and unfortunately, most of that life was spent in the streets. I'll consider it my atonement."

I hugged him tightly, as I started to cry.

"You don't have to do this. We can come up with something to fix this." I pleaded.

"No, Tae. No more plans, no more cleanups, and no more running."

I started crying even harder.

"You'll be fine. You have Trell here to protect you now. You don't need me anymore."

"You're the closest thing to a father I've ever had. You're supposed to be walking me down the aisle."

He wiped a tear from his eye. This was the first time I'd ever seen him cry, and it made me feel even worse. I hugged him again, and he kissed me on my forehead.

"I love you, baby girl." He said, "No matter where I am, I'm never too far away. Since you've been born, you've been my everything. I need you to stay strong for your family, and stay the hell out of trouble."

We both laughed as we broke our embrace.

"I have been a lot of trouble lately, haven't I?"

"Just like your damn daddy," he replied.

"I'm gonna come visit you all the time." I said.

"You better, and I better have money on my books too." He joked.

We hugged one last time before I got out of the car. I began sobbing as I watched him pull out of my driveway. I loved him for everything he'd done for me over the years, and whatever he needed from here on out, I would take care of. Not too many people, relative or not, would sacrifice their life for you, and I was more than grateful for him.

My mother always told me that when it came to success you would pay on the front end or the back end. I was surely paying on the back end. Sure, I could finally live in peace, but it was at the expense of my uncle. I was distraught right now, but I needed to get it together like I knew he wanted me to. So I quit crying, took a deep breath, and went inside my home to be the strong woman my family needed me to be.

## EPILOGUE

### One Year Later

I looked at myself in the mirror, and admired the work Dani did on my hair. I hated long hair, but I loved the sea of curls she had all over my hair. My makeup on the other hand, was pissing me off. I hired a makeup artist for the day, but I wasn't impressed with what she did. Everyone kept telling me that it looked fine, but it didn't look right to me. I kept trying to fix it, but I couldn't get it to look right. I knew that we were pressed for time, but I wanted everything to be perfect.

"Tae, please get dressed," my mother begged.

"Ma, I'm trying to fix this mess on my face."

"Taela, you look beautiful," she insisted. "You need to just chill out, and get dressed so we start on time."

"It's my wedding, they can wait."

"Let's go Tae," Dani chimed in. "We gotta be at the reception hall by nine."

"I don't know why ya'll would decide to get married so late." My mom said.

"It's New Year's Eve, Ma." I explained, "You can't have a New Year's Eve wedding during the day."

"I hear you, but it's past my damn bedtime," she said. "I'm too old for this."

Before I could argue with her, Dani jumped in.

"We can talk about this later," she said. "Tae, put the makeup down and get dressed."

I sighed, and put down my beauty blender. At this point it was going to be what it was, and I needed to get dress so I could go down the aisle.

"Ya'll know the drill. I need to be helped into this thing." I said.

My mother and Dani came over to help me in to my dress with caution. They had been trying to get me to calm down all morning, but it was easier said than done. The road to matrimony for Trell and I had been a long tumultuous one. Even after I found out that Aylin was lying about the baby, it was hard for me to trust him. Then we decided to push back the wedding while we went through all the legal stuff for Uncle Leon.

Last year, Uncle Leon pled guilty to four counts of first-degree murder. He took responsibility for the murders of Shaun, King, Angie, and Envy. He was sentence to live with the possibility of parole in twenty years. We were hoping that if he stayed out of trouble in there, we could try to lessen his mandatory years. They sent him to the Jessup Correctional Center back home in Maryland, and I made sure to visit him at least once a month. Every time I saw him he seemed to be in good spirits, but I don't think he would let me know if something was wrong.

He never wanted me to worry about him, but I did. I tried seeing the positive side of what he's done for me but it was hard. Today was especially hard for me because I wanted him to walk me down the aisle. There wasn't a day that went by where I didn't think about him, and I wished he could be here how Somaiya has grown. Once she was a little older, I would take her to see him but we both agreed that she was too young right now.

Somaiya was eighteen months, and she had the best little personality. She was super laid back and chill like her father, but she had my feistiness and strong will when she wanted to. Our love for her, the desire to have the family unit we didn't have growing up was a big factor in us getting right with each other. When I was younger, I always thought that love would be enough to make a relationship work, but to be with someone long term you needed more than that. You also needed commitment, dependability, communication, and trust. It took us going through the fire, for me to understand that.

As I stood in the back of the church with my mother and Dani, I was a nervous wreck. Since my uncle couldn't be here, I wanted my mother to give me away. It was only right, since she'd been there for me through everything. I also kept my party small, and just had Dani as my maid of honor. Of course, it was originally supposed to be her, Angie, and Envy. As crazy as it sounds, I missed them both, and I hated that it turned out the way it did. Dani took the news on Envy's betrayal and passing pretty hard, but she didn't know the details. She only knew what was in my uncle's deposition. I didn't know if she would be able to handle the full truth.

When the doors of the church opened slightly so that Dani could go in, I started shaking. There was no doubt that I wanted to spend the rest of my life with

Trell, but I was still nervous. My mother could feel me trembling, and put her arm around me.

"If you don't wanna do this, we can leave now," she whispered in my ear,

"I'm okay," I replied.

Just then the doors opened again, except this time they opened all the way. I almost cried when I saw Trell tear up at the altar. Although I tried to play it off, I knew from the first time I saw him that I was going to be with him. As I walked down the aisle, my anxiety turned into excitement. It was finally starting to set in that I was about to become Mrs. La' Trell Livingston. So many times, I wanted to ask someone to pinch me to see if I was dreaming. I never imagined my soulmate wasn't the man I'd spent most of my adult life in a relationship with, but a stranger from down south.

As I approached the altar, I was in awe of everything. The church was decorated with gold and black everywhere, and our small wedding party looked great. Personally, I was still shocked that we'd actually pulled it off; the decorations and the wedding itself. Even after all the wrong I'd done, God still blessed me with an amazing husband and daughter. He was exactly what I needed, and I'm glad I took a chance on him. I knew that I could be stubborn sometimes, and I wasn't that great at listening to people. Trell knew that, and has so patient and loving while I got my shit together.

When my mom and I got to the altar, the pastor started speaking. At the end of his speech, she gave me away and the ceremony began. I could barely listen to the pastor, because I was so focused on Trell. When it was time to say their vows, Trell went first.

"Taela, I loved you from the first time I saw you. You dissed me in my store, but there was something about you I couldn't let go. You always try to put on an act like you're so tough, but I see the real you." He said, "You're loving, caring, and supportive and I couldn't ask for a better partner. You and Somaiya are the best things to ever happen to me, and I promise to love and take care of you both forever."

I replied, "La' Trell you helped me through some of the lowest moments of my life. I don't know where I would be without you right now. It's funny how the one person I kept pushing away, is the person I'll be spending the rest of my life with. You've endured so much just to be with me and the fact that you never gave up on me, lets me know that I can always count on you. I promise to love you, cherish you, and be patient with you for the rest of our lives."

I thought about everything I'd been through over the past few years. I was the definition of the word survivor, and no one could take that away from me. How many women could say that they took the same situation I was in and made it out alive? I'd accomplished everything I'd ever dreamed of and even got a few added bonuses. I never thought I would have life after Shaun, and here I was.

I turned around and looked at my mother, who was holding Somaiya and smiled. Everything in my life was finally the way it should be, and even though I didn't take the straight path here, I didn't regret any of it. I was grateful for the mistakes, the lessons, and the losses. All of those things led me to this very moment, and without them, I'm not the woman I am today.

## ABOUT THE AUTHOR

S. Miller is a young author out of Maryland who specializes in African American fiction novels. As a high school student, she often found herself caught up in the plot and characters of many books in the genre, and was inspired to write short stories of her own. Her favorite author is Carl Weber. As a writer, her goal is to tell the stories of people in the African American community through characters that come from all walks of life.

CPSIA information can be obtained
at www.ICGtesting.com
Printed in the USA
LVHW041513111019
633943LV00011B/389/P